"Why on e........ .... him when I wasn't even married to him?"

Mother and daughter looked at each other across the room, the mother with genuine surprise, the daughter with horror.

"I'll get my own back on him," the mother said. "He'll be sorry he ever crossed my path by the time I get finished with him."

"Mother, I'm sure we can manage without the money. We've got each other."

Effie glanced at her strangely. "No, my dear, this has freed me from you and Johnnie. You can go back to your father now."

"But that is impossible!" Kitty stiffened into revolt. "It would be a dreadful shock to Johnnie to discover now that Father was...the sort of man who had tricked you into thinking that he could not marry you."

"Tricked me? Nobody tricked *me,* I assure you, my dear! I knew exactly what I was doing."

KITTY

Mary Ann Gibbs

FAWCETT COVENTRY • NEW YORK

A Fawcett Coventry Book

Published by Ballantine Books

Copyright © 1965 by Mary Ann Gibbs
Copyright © 1974 by Mary Ann Gibbs

ISBN 0–449–50301–1

Originally published as The Sugar Mouse by Hurst and Blackett in England, and by Beagle Books in the U.S.A.

Manufactured in the United States of America

First Ballantine Books Edition: July 1982
10 9 8 7 6 5 4 3 2 1

1

White Cliff Bay had never been a place to attract many visitors, and the day-trippers that thronged excursion trains to Brighton were unknown on its beaches. That was why it had a select type of resident, and in the summer months a few families from the better London suburbs rented furnished houses there.

The Ralstons came to it year after year, and the children loved it. Their father was never able to accompany them, but that was not unusual: so many of the visitors' breadwinners were professional men, or the owners of large businesses which it was not possible to leave for very long.

In the High Street of the little wind-swept town, shops catered for the needs of residents and visitors alike. The draper's, Spicer's, had ties that could be bought for sixpence, and lining for straw hats, cut on the cross, and ladies' black open-work stockings for evening functions. There was the butcher's shop, where Mr. Fry was usually to be found behind his chopping block, with his straw hat on his head and the blue striped apron that made him look even larger than he was, tied round his middle, and Mr. Twiddle, the greengrocer next door, his hands smelling of earth and onions as he cut bananas from the big stalks that hung there, and weighed out gooseberries in his battered scoop.

There was a stationer's, too, where the children bought comic papers and fairy stories in pink paper covers, and transfers for wet days, and books like *The Gorilla Hunters* and *What Katy Did* for one and sixpence, and new cedarwood pencils, and boxes of paints with small brushes included for fourpence, and painting books with large drawings to be coloured, the blank pages between to be filled with their own pictures of the Channel steamers that passed on the horizon twice a day.

There was the jeweller, Mr. Ponting, who had trays of mosaic brooches for souvenirs, priced at ninepence, and gunmetal watches for half-a-crown, and the grocer's shop, with a glorious spicy smell coming out of its doors, and the dairy with butter in wooden tubs and milk in shining, brass-bound pails, pint and half-pint measures hooked to their sides, and baskets of new-laid eggs at tenpence a score. And on the corner, next to the ironmonger's and marking the end of High Street before you turned into Broad Street, was a little sweet-shop, with pink sugar mice in the window, and humbugs, large and striped and cushiony, in tall glass jars.

Broad Street was a superior thoroughfare, accommodating the bank and the bank manager's house, and Doctor Bates's surgery, and Mr. Webber, the lawyer, and the Queen's Hall, where concerts were given in the summer and subscription dances held in the winter. There was only one shop in Broad Street, the baker's at the far end, full of fragrant new loaves, and freshly baked ha'penny buns, the step of the shop worn down in the middle by the feet that had gone up and down it over a hundred years.

When they reached the baker's Kitty and Johnnie Ralston knew they were not far from the sea. The salty smell that was never absent from the town became stronger and fresher, and the wind began to sigh in their ears and tear at the hair under their hats, so that the elastic under their chins grew taut as the brims were whipped back from their faces.

Down Fish Lane they would go, past the second-hand furniture shop at the bottom and up the other side, hurrying now in case somebody said something to stop them, such as, "Just a moment, dears, before we go on the beach. I have to buy some post-cards." Past the last shop in the Lane they would run without a glance for the black-soled sand-shoes that were tied up there in clusters over bundles of wooden spades, as if Mr. Twiddle's bananas had turned black overnight and grown a wooden stem, or the galvanised buckets stacked one inside the other on the shop floor, or the umbrella stand full of shrimping nets, or the table that held the revolving rack of post-cards. Across the empty road they would scamper, and there on the other side was the sea, spread out before them, tossing its waves into the sunshine as if it was tossing them at their feet, and they would halt on the parade in ecstasy, listening to the pounding shock of the waves on the shore, and the sharp intake of the receding water as the pebbles rushed after it, hissing their protest before another wave came to bring them rolling helter-skelter back again.

The Ralstons were earlier than usual that year, because the children had had whooping cough, and the doctor had advised Effie to take them to the sea. A furnished house with the grand name of Balmoral, in Saxe-Coburg Avenue, had been rented for three months, and off they went to it in early May, taking with them Mrs. Tapper the cook, Simpson the parlourmaid, Elsie the scullery-maid, and the boy Joe, and the fact that lessons still had to be done every day did not interfere with the delight of being there.

One day the children's mother had an old friend to visit her from Brighton: Maidie Burke was staying there with young Sidney while her husband, Wallie, was on tour as leading comedian in a theatrical com-

7

pany in the Midlands, and although Sidney was older than the Ralstons he had no objection to joining them in their afternoon walk over the headland with their governess.

Kitty led the way, sure-footed as a deer, out-pacing Sidney's longer and more leisurely stride, while nine-year-old Johnnie toiled behind, shouting at them to stop. Poor Miss Childs brought up the rear, pausing every now and then to look back at the ugly little town as an excuse to get her breath.

At the top of the headland Kitty stopped and faced into the wind. It was strong enough up there to deafen her, so that she had to shout to make herself heard, and when she took off her hat there was nobody to tell her to put it on again in case she caught a cold in her head. There was nobody either to tell her not to sit on the grass, as it was sure to be damp at this time of year, and she flung herself down on the turf, and Sidney sat down beside her, hugging his stockinged knees, a large expanse of shirt cuff showing below the sleeves of his Norfolk jacket, because he was growing out of his clothes faster than his mother could afford to buy them.

For a long moment they gazed down at the town, straggling along beside the shore and falling back here and there where marshy land made building impossible. Seen from that distance a horse and cart, travelling along the white curve of the chalky road to the harbour on the far side of the bay, looked a speck, its progress as slow as a snail. The houses in the town it had left were toys, the church a small grey stone box in the middle of them, the train in the station a clockwork one, waiting to be wound up when somebody found the key.

"I think," Kitty said, "that I love White Cliff Bay more than anywhere else in the world. I wish I could live there always, don't you?"

Sidney was not so sure. "I haven't seen many other places yet," he pointed out. "And I might like others better."

"You couldn't possibly." Kitty spread her hands in

8

the soft turf on either side of her, her fingers digging into the wild thyme and the close rosettes of the thistles, and the grasses that never stopped shaking in the wind. "Why, sitting up here like this makes you feel like..."

"God?" said Sidney cheerfully.

"Certainly not!" She spoke with dignity. "I was going to say that it made me feel like Gulliver looking down at Lilliput."

Sidney had no opinion of Lilliput. "Funny little Kitty," he said teasingly. "Full of dreams out of the story books. A quiet little creature too... like a mouse. One of those pink sugar mice in your sweet-shop here. I'll buy you one before I go home, if I've got any pocket-money left."

The sound of the wind beating in their ears seemed to shut them into a world of their own, in which they were peculiarly alone. It must be a lonely business, Kitty thought, to be Gulliver...to be God. She shivered, and picking a tinker-tailor grass began to tell her fortune.

"Tinker, tailor, soldier, sailor, rich man, poor man..." She threw the grass away. "It always comes to 'poor man' for me!"

"Better than 'beggarman' or 'thief'." He took up the grass, stripped it of its seeds, and put its stalk into her mouth. "See who gets to the middle first, you or me!" he said, and putting the other end in his own mouth began to nibble his way towards her. She watched his blue eyes and his mouth getting nearer and nearer her own, and then Johnnie's voice reached them as he came up to the last bit of the hill, and she dropped her end of the grass.

"Cheat!" Sidney said.

"Kitty dear!" gasped Miss Childs. "Your hat!...Put it on and get up off the grass at once. This is May, dear, not July!"

As Kitty scrambled up obediently and put on her hat Sidney got to his feet more slowly. "Does it make you feel like Gulliver, Miss Childs?" he asked, nodding at the town.

Miss Childs looked back with a wry smile. "Not at all. White Cliff Bay is, in my opinion, a very ugly little town, spoiling a nice stretch of shore. Come along, dears! It is time we went back to tea."

The young Ralstons ran on down the slope, leaving her to follow, which she did with aching ankles and a hat that threatened to be blown over the headland. She was grateful to Sidney for giving her a hand down the steeper parts where the turf path had been worn down to the chalk.

She had been feeling a great deal older since the death of the old Queen in January. To her, as to others who had grown to middle-age and beyond it in that one reign, it had seemed like the end of the world, and lately she had thought of changing to a less exacting post, where young people did not expect her to scramble tirelessly up and down hills, and be blown about by north-east winds on a front that had not even a band-stand.

Kitty, stopping half-way down the hill for them to catch her up, was conscious that the wind had suddenly slackened and the noise of it had stopped. It was possible now to hear the larks, and the mournful cry of the gulls, wheeling over the cliff edge, and the distant thud of the waves as they struck the rocks below, thrusting the spray into the air. She looked back at the top of the headland with a small feeling of aversion: up there she had felt frighteningly remote and alone, as if at any moment she might step off the world into the sky. It was far more comfortable to be down here, or further down still, in the warmer streets of the town, full of friendly faces and kindly voices and shop windows with fascinating things to buy.

"The Mouse is dreaming again," said Sidney, catching her up and leaving Miss Childs to walk the last part of the way by herself. "The Sugar Mouse with the chocolate eyes, the black cotton whiskers, the tail made of string…"

10

"I am not a sugar mouse," said Kitty, "and I have no tail made of string."

"Have you not? What's this then?" He gave her dark pigtail a gentle pull. "Come on, Johnnie! The sweetshop lies ahead of us.... Which will you have, a sugar mouse for a penny, or four bulls' eyes at a farthing each?"

Johnnie said he would have the bull's eyes. He believed in getting value for money. "But I'll have to hide them from Miss Childs," he added. "She thinks they are vulgar.... And we aren't allowed boiled sweets because one of her pupils nearly choked himself to death over one, nor chocolate because it spoils our meals."

"I'll buy her some acid drops," said Sidney consolingly. "It seems the obvious choice for your Miss Childs!"

Kitty took her pink sugar mouse home with her, but she did not eat it. It was far too beautiful. She found a little box for it and packed it up in tissue paper and when she got back to London she put it away in a drawer where she kept all her treasures: a lucky charm from the Christmas pudding, a dried sprig of white heather that her father had given her, a handkerchief containing a collection of sea-shells, and a few coloured pebbles that somehow lost their glow and transparency when they were taken from the beaches where they belonged.

2

On the afternoon that Effie Ralston sat in the ugly
drawing-room in Balmoral House talking to Maidie
Burke over tea, in a country village in East Anglia
Stephen Ralston Brett was walking across the park to
Cranston Place from the church, where he had been
taking part in a memorial service for his cousin Toby.

Outwardly correct in his frock coat and silk hat, his
lean, handsome face composed in an expression of gravity to befit the occasion, his heart could not avoid a
small leap of excitement as his eyes rested on the old
house that was now his.

Cranston Place had always been more important
than anything else to the men of the Brett family, with
the exception of poor young Toby, who had foolishly
put his Queen and Country first and died in South
Africa, a victim to the enteric that had claimed so many
of Britain's soldiers.

There had been Bretts at Cranston for more than
four hundred years, and it had taken not a little man-
agement and skill to stay there at times, especially

during the Civil War when a gentleman was expected to declare either for King or Parliament and to die for his beliefs while his house went up in flames behind him.

Fortunately for Stephen, Toby had been too young to marry before he joined the Yeomanry, and the estate had passed to a man who appreciated it fully. He intended to settle down for life at Cranston as his family had done before him.

"You will be staying, sir?" asked Newsome the butler when he arrived, but it was scarcely a question.

"I shall be staying," Stephen said firmly.

"Thank you, sir. We all hoped you would. I have had the late master's bedroom prepared for you. Mrs. Hobbs thought that was what you would like."

"Mrs. Hobbs was right."

His uncle's bedroom had never been used by his cousin Toby. It was a large, sombre apartment, furnished in heavy mahogany, on its walls prints of some of the better known of the family portraits. Several of these portraits bore Stephen's own features and dark eyes: a fact that was strikingly evident to the family when he received them in the north drawing-room—a cold, dark room reserved for mournful occasions such as this.

Not many of his relatives had been able to come. His Aunt Mary had driven over from Burgeston Hall with her thin, spinster daughter Emily, and her companion, Miss Long, and his Aunt Ellen had come by train from London, accompanied by his cousin Lionel and his two schoolboy sons, Ernest and Walter, and Stephen's only sister, Sophie Cartwright, whose arrogance and domineering ways had sent a mild little husband to an early grave.

The little church had been filled mostly by farmers and employees on the estate, the front pews being reserved for the family and male members of neighbouring county families, coming out of affection for Toby, who had been popular with everybody, and curiosity

13

to see how the new owner was reacting to his unexpected inheritance.

"Of course," said Lady Burgeston, adding two lumps of sugar and some cream to the cup of tea on the footman's tray, "you will have to marry now, Stephen. There must be no more of this gay bachelor life: it is your duty to marry and give the family an heir." She glanced sharply at the nervous young man in front of her. "Did I put two lumps in that cup or three, James?"

"Two, I think, m'lady."

"You only think?...Then I'd better take another. Well, Stephen, what have you got to say?"

"He's got nothing to say, Mary," said her sister Ellen sharply, "because he may please himself. With Lionel and his two boys here the Place won't be without an heir, if Stephen likes to remain a bachelor to the day of his death."

Stephen studied them thoughtfully over his tea. He had no intention of allowing Lionel or his sons to enter the Place except as his guests, and in his opinion his Aunt Mary was right. It was his duty to marry, but he would take his time. He could afford to pick and choose, and there were other things to be settled first.

He made his way round the family, receiving their congratulations with a gravity that did not deceive them.

"Poor old Toby," he said again and again. "It was bad luck, dear old fellow.... Very bad luck indeed."

Only his sister showed him unkindly that she saw through him. "That's what comes of being patriotic," she said with a short laugh. "*You* never had any urge to fight, had you, Stephen?" And she took a silver case from her pocket and lighted a cigarette to lend emphasis to her words and to shock her aunts. This she succeeded in doing.

"My dear!" said Lady Burgeston. "In the drawing-room!"

"Do it good to fumigate it," Sophie said. "Place smells like a morgue."

"Sophie should have been a man, Aunt Mary," said

14

Stephen blandly. "She would have made a good one, even if she has no manners."

"At least," said Sophie, "I'd be in South Africa at this moment—not hanging about at home letting better men go in my place."

The family were accustomed to this edged bickering between Stephen and his sister: they knew it meant nothing and that there was quite a strong bond of affection between them. While she enjoyed her cigarette he went on to speak to the estate's agent, Harold Alcot, and to tell him that he would be ready to start going through the accounts with him on the following day.

"I should be obliged if you will be here by eleven o'clock," he said, making the request sound like an order, and Harold Alcot flushed.

"I can be here any time you wish, Mr. Brett," he said, and finished his tepid tea and left the family alone while he went home to report on his new employer to his wife.

"I'll tell you one thing, Amy," he said. "The family doesn't like him."

"I don't care a scrap about the family," she said. "The only thing that concerns me is whether you like him, darling!"

"I don't know." He thought it over. "I'd have preferred Mr. Lionel—he's got twice the humanity of his cousin. But I daresay Mr. Stephen will be easier to work with than young Toby. *He* was as difficult to pin down as an eel! 'Do as you like, Alcot,' he'd say. 'You know more about it than I do.' And off he'd go to enjoy himself in Scotland or Leicestershire or London, or wherever the fancy took him. Mr. Stephen will want to see every i dotted and every t crossed, but I am a meticulous man myself, and I like orderliness where an estate as big as this is concerned. But the man himself strikes me as being slightly inhuman, and don't ask me why because I don't know. It was merely an impression I had. He seems to me to be the sort of chap who would never lose his head over anything or any-

15

body. Even his affections would be made to serve his purpose."

"He sounds a cold fish!" Amy gave a small shiver. "No wonder you don't like him." And then she changed the subject to that of her son's first tooth, which had been cut the day before and was a great deal more interesting to his fond mamma than Mr. Stephen Ralston Brett.

The family did not stay long. Lady Burgeston was the first to go, and Ellen and Lionel and his sons left soon afterwards. Sophie was staying the night before taking part in a Ladies' Golf Tournament on the following day at Yarmouth.

"Well," she said, coming into the library where her brother had retreated. "Here you are at last, Stephen — master of Cranston Place."

"Yes." He drew in his breath. "Nobody can take it from me now." There was satisfaction in his voice and Sophie's thoughts went for a fleeting second to Toby, young, gay and lighthearted, turning his back on his duty to the family to go hunting Boers in South Africa as he would have gone deer-stalking in Scotland or fox-hunting in Leicestershire. She asked curiously: "Do you intend to live here on your own?"

"At first. There will be a great deal to see to, because Uncle Richard did not look after things as he should, and Toby was not master here long enough to care. Why do you ask?"

"Not from any ulterior motive, my dear! I have no wish to act as your hostess here. I have never liked the Place, as you know."

"Nevertheless, as you are my only sister I do offer it to you as your home, Sophie. You are welcome to regard it as such as long as you like."

"Thank you." She was gratified by his thought for her. "I must say I like the village. It is pretty and the people are respectful, and have a great regard for the family. I would not mind having Mrs. Lestrange's little house later on, if another could be found for her."

"And who is Mrs. Lestrange?"

"A charming widow, in whom our Uncle Richard had a considerable interest. Oh, there was nothing scandalous in their association. He was simply a great friend of her husband's, and knowing that she had been left badly off he offered her Ivy Lodge, and she was thankful to accept the offer. She is a very nice woman, and her two children are handsome and popular in the neighbourhood."

"But you would like her house, all the same?"

She shrugged her shoulders. "There is no hurry. I am content with my London flat, especially if I can come and stay here from time to time. I presume you intend to marry, Stephen?"

"Certainly. But like yourself, I shall not be in a hurry."

"Have you anybody in mind?" His sister's expression became more interested. "It isn't the little woman in St. John's Wood?"

"No." He frowned. "Of course not."

"How will you get rid of her?"

"That is my business, I think."

"Well yes, so it is. But I hope you won't be too brutal about it. I remember seeing her on the stage years ago, when you were first running after her, and I thought she was a fascinating little thing. I could not understand how she could have been persuaded to give up a promising career on your account, especially as there was a rumour going round at the time that the great Calverley Ricketts wanted to marry her!"

"My dear Sophie, you are scarcely a fit person to judge in such matters." There was a touch of superiority in Stephen's frosty smile. "Effie is a nice little woman, but she is nobody of importance, and I daresay even Ricketts realised that in the end. I would not dream of marrying her, and she knows it. So let's say no more about it, if you please. It is not a subject that I care to discuss with my sister."

"As you choose. I hope though for all our sakes that she will not come here and make a scene."

"That, my dear, is very unlikely to happen."

"I'm glad you are so sure of it!" And with this parting shot she went away to dress for dinner.

Left to himself Stephen walked restlessly to the empty fireplace, where his eye was caught and held by the portrait of young Toby over the chimney piece. As he studied it a feeling of bleakness came over him and he felt older than his forty years. He would have it put in the gallery directly he had another to take its place. A portrait of himself, perhaps, or of his wife, when he had one. He saw it there, painted by Sargent, a tall woman, young and handsome, with a smiling mouth and serene eyes, and a dress of some lace material, with flowing sleeves and a graceful skirt....

He was annoyed with Sophie for having brought up the unwelcome subject of Effie Fotheringay. Something would have to done about her, of course, and the sooner the better. Unpleasant duties did not become less so from being postponed. He had no wish to go and see her himself: the best thing he could do, he thought, frowning at young Toby who laughed back at him from his canvas with heartless joy, was to put the whole thing in the hands of his solicitors. Fanshawe would know what to do: he was a man of the world, and knew all about Effie. He would tell him that he was prepared to make a generous settlement, and after receiving the lawyer's letter she was not likely to make trouble.

For a second he remembered her wide grey eyes, the slender wings of her brows above them, and her ready laughter, and his heart almost misgave him. Then as he remembered some of her friends his mouth hardened.

There was Calverley Ricketts for one, conceited, successful, sneering and insolent: he had never forgiven him for stealing Effie from him. And there was that fat, vulgar comedian who appeared on the music halls, with a thin little wife who had nothing to say and a young son, Sidney, who had far too much. No Effie Fotheringay could be mistress of Cranston Place: it needed somebody with dignity and breeding and grace....

On the following morning, after Sophie had gone, he

sat down and wrote his letter to Mr. Fanshawe, putting the matter to him shortly and unemotionally. Then he directed and stamped it, and walked with it to the village post office, instead of leaving it with the other letters on the hall tray. There was a pleasantly final sound about the thud with which it dropped into the post box, as if it ended an interlude in his life which had latterly become more wearisome than pleasant.

About a week later Effie Ralston left the children at White Cliff Bay with Miss Childs and went back to London for a few nights.

"It is a business visit," she told the governess. "My husband's lawyer wants to see me about a rather urgent matter. I can't think what it is, unless I have been spending too much money in Mr. Ralston's absence! But the children grow so fast that I always seem to be buying new clothes for them—especially boots! I suppose you cannot expect a London lawyer to understand things like that though."

"But the house is shut up!" cried Miss Childs. "How will you manage?"

"I shall take Simpson with me. As I shall be by myself there will be nothing for her to do, except get my meals."

"Your husband will not be at home then?"

"No," said Effie. "Mr. Ralston will not be at home."

The children went to the station to see their mother off, and while they walked up the platform to admire the fussy little engine with its tall black smoke stack, and the cab where the driver and his mate waited for the wave of the green flag to send them on their way, Effie sent Simpson ahead with a porter and the luggage and went into the telegraph office to despatch a telegram.

As she hurried down the platform after the children Miss Childs was very much afraid that she knew to whom the telegram was being sent. In her opinion Mr. Calverley Ricketts was too frequent a visitor to Mr. Ralston's house during the long periods when its mas-

19

ter was away from home. She wondered if these visits could have had anything to do with the lawyer's peremptory summons to Mrs. Ralston, because, while her mind shuddered away from the thought of divorce, she could not help remembering that Mrs. Ralston had been on the stage, too, at one time of her life.

And while there was no doubt that the majority of actors and actresses led blameless lives and worked very hard in their profession, their free and easy manners made one think that they might be more Bohemian in their ideas than other people.

Miss Childs felt she could go no further than that, even in her thoughts, but as she stood with the children waving to the back of the departing train a few minutes later, she told herself once more that it was time she made a change.

3

The houses in Willowbroook Road were discreetly respectable, the steps leading up to the front doors above
the areas as white as snow, the lace curtains all down
the road hanging with an exact precision as if Simpson
had gone from house to house that morning, settling
them straight in the windows.

As his hansom cab turned into the road that afternoon in May, Calverley Ricketts remembered how Effie
had once remarked that she thought the aspidistras
and the palms behind the curtains were washed off once
a week with milk, and when he asked if she washed
her asparagus fern with the same liquid she had shaken
her golden head at him and laughed.

"My dear Cal, what a question! When you've been
brought up in childhood to treat every drop of milk as
if it were a drop of gold, you don't waste it on ferns—
even skimmed milk at a penny a pint!"

Number 47 was on the corner and had a bigger garden than the others. Tall trees grew there, convenient
for the swing that was attached to a massive branch,

and lilacs and laburnums bloomed there, too, giving it an air of the country. Not that Ricketts cared: if Effie had lived in a tenement he would have gone to see her just the same because he was in love with her.

As the cab drew near the house he straightened the carnation in his buttonhole, flicked an imaginary speck of dust from his sleeve with a carefully trained gesture, and set his silk hat at a more jaunty angle. Looking at him, anybody would have known that he was a successful actor, always conscious of an audience.

The cab stopped and he told the cabby to wait, and mounted the steps. The house was quiet, and Simpson admitted him with a smile of welcome.

Effie was waiting for him in her little drawing-room and came to him with hands outstretched. She was a very pretty woman still, with the lovely profile that had first caught his eye and ensnared his heart, and a slender figure that showed off the gay dresses she loved to wear.

"My dear, dear Cal!" she cried. "I thought you were never coming!"

He took her hands and raised them to his lips. "I'd have been here sooner if the streets hadn't been up everywhere. They always seem to wait for the beginning of the summer to pick them up, nobody knows why."

"Oh, Cal!" She tried to smile but her eyes filled.

"What's happened?" He kept her hands in his. "Effie!...That telegram...was there something behind it?"

"Not when I sent it. I'd had a letter from old Fanshawe asking me to come and see him, but I thought it was because I'd overspent the quarter's allowance. Until I saw him this morning I'd no idea it could be...anything else...."

"But now..."

"Now..." She freed herself gently and walked to the window that overlooked the garden at the back of the house and stared down blindly at the swing and the flower borders and the lilacs. "Stephen wants to put an end to our life together...he has grown tired of me...."

"So that's it!" There was a note of exultation in his voice. "Well, I warned you from the start that this would happen, my dear, but you wouldn't listen."

"He'd been to see me so seldom lately," she went on plaintively, "that I suppose I should have known that the break was coming, but somehow I didn't."

"You have always under-estimated his character, my dear. I knew exactly what he was capable of when you first set up house with him."

"I know, and you weren't the only one. My mother—you remember how she was a dresser in the theatre for years—she said to me at the time, 'If it's marriage you're after, Effie, keep to your own kind. Gentlemen like Stephen Brett don't marry actresses.' They didn't when she was a girl, but they seem to have altered their ways since. There have been quite a few lords who have married Gaiety girls recently, Cal!"

"Ah, but the landed gentry have to be more careful than the peerage, my dear! They have to consider their position...I hope Brett has been generous with you, that's all."

She shrugged her shoulders. "Mr. Fanshawe seemed to think he had, but that's according to how you look at it. He is allowing me three thousand a year, but not for myself alone. Oh, dear no! Two thousand of that is for the children, and only the remaining thousand for myself! He could have given me six without missing it, especially since he has come into his cousins' estate."

"Ah, yes, I saw something about it in the newspapers. Cranston wasn't it, in Norfolk? Would you like me to go up there and give him a thrashing? My hands have been itching to get on to him for years."

"He'd only sue you for assault, and I would get nothing then. As Mr. Fanshawe so righteously pointed out, I've no legal claim on him." She added bitterly: "It is all so like Stephen. He always did think he could get rid of his responsibilities by paying out cheques, and now he still doesn't give a thought to my side of the

23

affair—to the servants and Miss Childs and the neighbours, I mean. They all think I'm a respectable married woman—well, I've always *felt* as if I were married—and what am I to say to them now?"

"You can at least pack the children off to their father. They're his, as much as they are yours."

"Cal, I'm not joking!"

"And neither am I."

She glanced at his face. "No, I don't believe you are.... What I ought to have said was that I've got to think out some plausible story before I go back to White Cliff Bay and I'd hoped you might be able to suggest something."

He was unwilling to help. "What do people know about your supposed husband?" he said.

"That he is a wine merchant who has to travel abroad a great deal, and so far everyone has accepted it without question. I changed my name to Ralston by deed poll in the year that Kitty was born, and so I suppose legally the children are entitled to the name."

"I daresay." He frowned at the carpet. "Has Brett made any conditions?"

"Oh, yes, didn't I tell you?" She laughed angrily. "I'm to leave this house at once, and not attempt to write to him or to see him, or in fact to 'molest' him in any way! You might think I was a woman he'd picked up out of the streets!"

"Charming Mr. Brett, running true to form! But have you full control of the children's money?"

"Of the income only, until they are twenty-one. Then they will inherit the capital that is settled upon them."

"I see. How old is the elder child?"

"Kitty is thirteen."

"So that you have eight years in which to spend an income of three thousand pounds a year without having to account to anyone for a penny!" His eyes were alert. "It is not a fortune, but it might have been worse. What sort of a town is White Cliff Bay?"

She shrugged her shoulders. "I suppose you would call it select. The residents are mostly retired army

24

people, I believe, with a few titles scattered among them. Why do you ask?"

"Because it seems that it might be just the sort of place for the widow of one of our gallant Yeomanry officers to settle down in with her two children."

"A widow?" Her eyes began to sparkle. "Cal, what is in your mind? I can see by your face that you have thought of something!"

He chuckled. "It is only an idea as yet, but with careful thought it might do....It might do very well. The first thing you must insist upon is for Brett to visit you in White Cliff Bay next week for the purpose of saying goodbye to his wife and children before sailing for South Africa."

She shook her head. "He won't show his face down there! He's afraid of running into his sister: she plays in golf tournaments, you see."

"Then he must arrange his visit for a day when she is not playing golf, mustn't he? He has made conditions—very well you must make some in your turn."

"Me? Make conditions?" She began to laugh. "You don't know what you are talking about!"

"On the contrary, I know very well. Mr. Brett is not a man to invite the slightest breath of scandal, especially now that he has come into his large country estate. Gossip flies about in the country faster than it does in town, because people have only their neighbours to talk about." He took her by the shoulders and propelled her swiftly to her little desk. "Sit down, my dear, and take up your pen and write as I tell you."

His arrogance was comforting: she sat down obediently and after a moment's thought he dictated slowly:
"Dear Mr. Fanshawe,

After thinking things over since I left you this morning, I have decided to accept the terms imposed on me by Mr. Brett, but in return for this concession on my part and in view of the nature of our association, and the ages of our children, I feel that I should make some terms on their behalf, to be complied with by Mr. Brett. I suggest therefore that he should spend a day with us

25

in White Cliff Bay as early as possible, ostensibly to say goodbye before sailing for South Africa in one of the Yeomanry Regiments." Calverley smiled grimly as Effie gave an exclamation of protest. "I am not suggesting, my dear, that Brett *should* go to South Africa! I don't think he'd consent to anything like that!... Let me see, where had we got to?" He glanced over her shoulder. "Ah, yes... *'and at the end of June I must ask him to send me a telegram saying that my husband has been killed in action. On receipt of this telegram I will at once write to you, giving the undertaking he requires.'*" He stopped. "I think that should settle the matter, Effie."

"But supposing the South Africa War doesn't last another month?"

"My dear girl, it will drag on for a long time yet."

She sighed. "Oh, well, I daresay Mr. Fanshawe will pass the letter on to Stephen, but I don't suppose he will take any notice of it."

"Then we must make sure that he does." Calverley was brisk. "We can't threaten him, with a lawyer at the other end, but he must know that you mean what you say. So before you sign the letter, just put in one more paragraph, to the effect that if Mr. Brett finds it difficult to meet you in this matter, you suggest that you should bring the children and their governess to Cranston so that you can discuss everything at greater length. I think you will find that will do the trick. A man as selfish and proud as Brett is not going to risk having you and the children and that starchy governess arriving on his doorstep. He would find it difficult to explain you all to his friends and neighbours, quite apart from all the old retainers about the place!"

She gave an uncertain little laugh. "He might even feel forced to marry me, and think how humiliating that would be!"

He put a firm hand on her shoulder. "Now, Effie, I did not say that! But it is no good appealing to Brett's finer feelings, because he hasn't any. If he had he'd have married you years ago. I wanted to, God help me,

26

and I still would marry you, if it weren't for his damned brats. Much as I love their mother I'm hanged if I'm going to give them a home!"

She put her hands on his shoulders. "My poor Cal...will you ever forgive me?"

"I forgave you long ago...but I'll never forgive Brett." He covered her hands with his. "When you return to White Cliff Bay I suggest that you start looking for a house—preferably in an isolated position—that can be rented cheaply and run by one general servant. A widow, you see, might be expected to be left badly off..."

"But I don't think I want to live in White Cliff Bay."

"I am not suggesting that you should live there more than is absolutely necessary. But you must have a house for the children and their governess, and even if you have to pack them off to boarding school you should still have a couple of thousand to spend." He smiled down into her eyes. "I shall be delighted to help you to spend it...in Paris and elsewhere. And now, having settled that, tell me which theatre you would like me to take you to tonight? The new play doesn't open till next week, and tonight is all yours!"

As Effie was writing her letter that afternoon, Stephen Ralston Brett was taking a walk through the Rhododendron Ride at Cranston. The bushes were late in blooming that year, but they were now almost at their best, and as he strolled along, not hurrying because it was such a pleasant afternoon he heard the sound of voices ahead of him. In a few moments he drew level with one of the small paths that led off the Ride and saw three people there coming towards him. They all stopped when they saw him, and the older of the two ladies in the group gave an exclamation of distress.

"I think you must be Mr. Brett?" she said.

"I am." He raised his hat with a grave smile.

"Then we must introduce ourselves and apologise at the same time for trespassing! I am Mrs. Lestrange, and these are my daughter Muriel, and my son, Richard. Your uncle was Richard's god-father, and he gave us permission to use the Ride for our rambles, and as Toby continued his father's kindness I'm afraid we have fallen into the habit of behaving as if the Ride belonged to us. But we had been told that you were not in residence yet, and we came to say goodbye to it before Rick goes back to finish his first term at Sandhurst. He has been at home with a sprained wrist."

The young man said nothing. While his mother talked to the new owner, his eyes rested on Mr. Brett's coldly handsome face with some curiosity, comparing him unfavourably with Toby. But Stephen Brett was only vaguely conscious of his scrutiny: his attention had been arrested by Muriel, and he had no eyes for anyone else.

Tall, graceful and very lovely, she might have been picked by Providence to be the subject of the portrait that was to replace Toby's over the library chimney piece, and while he answered the mother politely he could only see the daughter.

He knew that he begged Mrs. Lestrange to continue her walk, and that he said he would not dream of interrupting their pleasure in the Ride, and asked them to go on regarding it as their own. But all the time he was speaking, it was Muriel to whom his words were addressed, and she did not even smile.

Mrs. Lestrange made up for her children's lack of warmth as she walked ahead with him, saying how delighted everyone was to know that he intended to make Cranston his home.

"Dear Toby was so seldom here," she confided sorrowfully. "He was so young and so—forgive me for saying this!—so scatterbrained! One never felt that the dear old Place meant anything to him."

She told him that her husband had been killed on the North-west Frontier in India, and that Richard Brett had written to her directly he heard the news, to offer her and her family a house in the village.

"He said it was so that he could keep an eye on his godson," she added. "But I knew it was because he was aware that I had been left with very little means." She hesitated and then went on, "When Toby inherited the Place I spoke to Mr. Alcot about Ivy Lodge, because I realised that the rent I was paying was ridiculously low, and recently I spoke to him again. He said he would discuss it with you at an early date."

"And no doubt he will do so, but in the meantime may I beg you not to worry your head about it, Mrs. Lestrange?" Stephen smiled down at the little lady reassuringly. "I am sure we can come to some agreement, and perhaps you will allow me to call on you about it a little later on?"

She said she would be pleased to see him. They came to the parting of the ways and waited for the young people to join them.

"Muriel has a key to the gates," said Mrs. Lestrange. "I think you should give it back to Mr. Brett now, dear."

The tall girl took the key from the pocket of her dress and held it out to the new owner. "I am happy to return your property, Mr. Brett," she said.

"Please keep it, Miss Lestrange." He waved it aside hurriedly. "No friend of my uncle's is to be shut out of the Ride by me."

She received it back uncertainly, a faint colour in her face as she thanked him, her thanks dying abruptly under her mother's effusiveness, and then they said goodbye and went on their way.

After tea, when Richard had gone off to have a few hours fishing with the Rector before nightfall, with a promise to guard his injured wrist, Mrs. Lestrange introduced the subject of Stephen Brett to her daughter. "Did she not think him a handsome man?" she wanted to know. "As handsome as poor Toby?"

Muriel did not reply and her mother went on: "People are saying that he intends to marry, which means that half the county will be after him, and I must say I think his wife will be a fortunate woman."

Muriel glanced at her mother with a cool little smile. "Why?" she asked.

"Well, my dear..." Mrs. Lestrange made a little

29

helpless gesture. "So charming...and so rich. For Mrs. Stephen Brett of Cranston Place there will be no managing with one general servant, no scrimping on food bills, no turning of dresses, no trimming up of old hats. She will have everything she wants, and a handsome husband into the bargain."

"Which might be more than she bargained for!" said Muriel dryly.

Her mother sighed and tried again. "I know that Toby meant a great deal to you...but you can't live on memories, my love. Sooner or later you will have to face the future, and I want it to be a good one for you, my darling."

"But give me time, dear." Muriel knelt down beside her mother and took her hand. "Don't throw rich husbands at my head until I am ready for them."

"It is only because I hate seeing you badly dressed and shabby," said her mother with tears in her eyes. "I want you to have your own carriage, I want so much for you, my love. Richard is a man, and he can fight for himself, especially with the money he will come into eventually from old Uncle Sam. But there's nothing for a girl in your position, Muriel. Nothing but marriage."

"I know." Muriel kissed her quickly and escaped to her own room, there to take out Toby's last letter and to read it through again, and wonder if she would ever be able to walk in the Ride without seeing him and hearing his voice, and feeling his careless kisses on her lips.

For to Toby everything had been a game to be enjoyed, even his love for her, and his service in South Africa.

"I am sitting outside my tent having breakfast," he wrote. *"It is a beautiful morning, although the night was cold, and I cannot say much for the cooking facilities in camp. We have been warned to take our tea and coffee without milk, and to avoid drinking water unless we know the sources to be pure, but you know me. The fever that seems to be picking out victims here and there will*

not get its claws into Toby Brett. He is too old a hand at camping for that."

Two days after writing that letter he was dead, and his cousin had stepped into his shoes. Muriel considered the new owner of the Place dispassionately: if love were not to be there as well, one husband, she supposed, was as good as another, and not all had a property as beautiful as Cranston. The man was confident, arrogant and assured, as if he usually got what he wanted, and if the time should come when he wanted her, should she not take what the gods offered and be thankful?

4

A copy of Effie's letter brought Stephen Brett to London in a towering rage.

"Didn't you make it clear to the woman that I do not intend to have anything further to do with her?" he demanded, storming his way into the lawyer's offices in Lombard Street.

"I am sure she understands the situation, Mr. Brett," said Mr. Fanshawe quietly.

"Then perhaps you will be able to explain what she means by this?" Stephen flung the letter down on his desk.

Mr. Fanshawe cleared his throat. "I was asked to forward the letter to you," he pointed out. "But as to what was meant in it I could not say, unless she feels that she would like your two children to regard their father more as a dead hero, than as somebody they might not be able to regard with such affection or respect."

"Of all the confounded impudence!" Mr. Brett scowled.

"If she intends to be difficult about it I shall have to put her in her place."

Mr. Fanshawe sighed. "I don't suppose she will carry out her declared intention of visiting you at Cranston," he remarked doubtfully. "It must have occurred to her that you would find it embarrassing. But one never quite knows what a woman will take it into her head to do if she fancies she has been slighted."

There was a short silence while each man thought of Effie's possible descent upon the Place, Mr. Fanshawe with dry amusement, Stephen Brett with undisguised horror. And as coupled with that picture, there came into the latter's mind the thought of the young woman living not a stone's throw from his gates, and the headway he had proposed making with her that summer, and what such an arrival in Cranston would mean to his chances, he left Mr. Fanshawe's offices even more furious than when he entered them.

He spent several hours walking about the streets, one half of his mind set against seeing Effie again, and the other half inclined to take the next train to White Cliff Bay. And eventually the second half won.

He arrived late in the afternoon, and as Simpson showed him into the dining room at Balmoral Effie jumped up from the tea table to welcome him.

"I know why you have come!" she cried. "You are on your way to Southampton! Oh, Stephen...my hero!"

She flung her arms round his neck and kissed him, enjoying to the full his expression of disgust, and then, keeping her arm in his, turned to face the surprised governess and bewildered children.

"I didn't tell you before, darlings," she said to the children, "but the reason why Father hasn't been to see us for so long is because he has been drilling with the Yeomanry on Salisbury Plain, haven't you, my love? He has been longing to get out to South Africa before the war ends."

Fortunately Stephen was freed from the necessity of speech by Kitty, who flung herself upon him.

33

"You have come to say goodbye!" she cried. "Oh, Father, why have you got to go?"

"Have you got a uniform?" asked Johnnie, ever practical. "And a sword? Can I see it?"

"I haven't brought it with me," muttered Stephen, more embarrassed and angry than he had been in his life. "And don't start weeping Kitty...there's nothing to cry about."

"B-but you may be killed!" The tears welled up slowly in Kitty's eyes. "We may never see you again!"

"He'll get the V.C. most likely," said Johnnie. "Are you the Colonel of the regiment, Father?"

"Not yet, darling," said Effie. "But he soon will be, won't you, my love?" Her eyes met his wickedly over Kitty's head, and Miss Childs saw the exchange of glances and was more puzzled than ever by her employer and his wife.

After he had gone, after staying barely an hour with them, Kitty was still the only one to grieve.

"I'd have dearly loved to see him in his uniform," she mourned. "He must look so splendid in it. And he stayed for such a little time."

Effie thought it extremely tiresome of the child to be so devoted to a man who cared nothing about any of them, and when she came upon her later on that evening in a corner of the ugly drawing-room, quietly weeping into an antimacassar in one of the horse-hair chairs, her impatience with her daughter got beyond her.

She walked on into the morning-room where Johnnie was setting out all the lead soldiers he had brought with him on the table, and playing at war with more enthusiasm than ever.

"This is Father's regiment," he told Effie excitedly. "And that is the enemy...this if Father on the white horse. He's the Colonel...when will Father be the Colonel, Mother?"

"I don't know." Effie's voice was sharp. "Miss Childs, Kitty is in the drawing-room, crying her eyes out."

"I'll go to her at once, Mrs. Ralston." The governess

34

got up quickly. "Poor little girl...She is so very sensitive!"

"I hope she will grow out of it then," snapped Effie. "She will never catch a husband by snivelling." And she went on up to her room.

Miss Childs hurried off indignantly. Every time she had seen Mrs. Ralston with her husband in the past year it had been plain that the poor man was becoming increasingly aware that he had married beneath him, and his visit this afternoon had confirmed it. He was such a perfect gentleman in every way, mourned Miss Childs, while his wife never made any secret of the fact that she had been on the stage. If she had been in such a situation she would have tried to keep it dark, and she would have put away some of the photographs that adorned the drawing-room walls in Willowbrook Road—notably the one of Mrs. Ralston as Rosalind, in those unfortunate tights. But no doubt Mr. Ralston had been like the rest of his sex, easily caught by a pretty face· ho had married in haste and was now repenting at leisure.

Her own duty was plain, however. Until he came home again she must do her best by his children, and having made up her mind on this point with a feeling of self-sacrifice, she was irritated to find that Kitty was weeping as much for that horrid boy, Sidney Burke, as she was weeping for her father, while her own offers of comfort were brushed aside.

"I wish Sid were here," sobbed Kitty. "He always knows how to comfort me."

"Well, he isn't here because he is at school," said Miss Childs sensibly. "And please call him Sidney, dear, not Sid. It is vulgar to shorten names."

"You don't like him," sniffed Kitty. "You've never liked him, and I don't know why. He only makes us laugh, and where is the harm in laughing?" And she gave way to a fresh burst of tears to give point to this remark.

"I don't dislike Sidney, dear, but he has a habit of ridiculing people, and it isn't kind."

"But he doesn't mean it unkindly!" Kitty sat up and wiped her eyes on the antimacassar. "It's only because they are funny that he does it.... Don't you remember how he took off the King that day, with a wool beard, and speaking half in German?... It was so funny!" She gave a watery smile at the memory.

"The King is the first gentleman in the land," said Miss Childs severely.

"But when we went to see Mr. Ricketts in *King Henry VIII* he was taking off a king, wasn't he?... And a dreadful king at that... And nobody saw any harm in it."

"Don't argue, dear," said Miss Childs. "It is bad manners."

But she was glad to see that the tears were finally driven from Kitty's eyes, and although her ankles were stiff from the walking they had already done that day, she gave her pupil a kiss and suggested that they should fetch Johnnie and go on the beach for a time before supper.

That night she wrote to her married sister in Dorset, telling her about Mr. Ralston's visit. *"Of course he only came to say goodbye before sailing for South Africa,"* she wrote. *"Mrs. Ralston is a very peculiar sort of woman, dear. She showed no emotion whatever after he was gone, and was angry with poor little Kitty for taking it to heart. I cannot make her out at all. Of course she is not a lady, and I am afraid the poor man bitterly regrets his marriage."*

Triumphant at the success of her letter to Stephen, Effie followed Calverley Ricketts's advice and began to look for an unfurnished house to rent in White Cliff Bay when her summer tenancy of Balmoral ran out at the end of June. She said nothing about her search to anybody in her household, and after looking at a number of houses that were either too large or too small or too expensive, she came upon a roomy old dwelling out on the Harbour Road that appeared to fulfil all her requirements.

It was called Flint House because it was built of flint,

36

and besides having the accommodation she wanted, it had a small, walled garden and a fine view of the harbour and the sea from the drawing-room windows. Because of its isolated position the rent was low, and although a strong smell of damp came to meet her when she opened the front door and the windows were almost obscured by salt from the spray that beat upon them most of the winter months, she decided to take it on a yearly tenancy.

At the end of June she took her family and servants back to Willowbrook Road to wait there for the telegram that would finally sever the tie with Stephen, but in Cranston Mr. Brett had forgotten that he had not yet finished the part that Effie had given him to play.

June was one of the loveliest months of the year at the Place: the trees in the park were every shade of green, from the tender pastel shade of beech to the heavy gold of oak, and the rose-gardens blossomed overnight. He had great baskets of roses sent down to Ivy Lodge, with hampers of young vegetables and strawberries, warm from the beds.

Under such open-handed bombardment Mrs. Lestrange smiled a welcome whenever he chose to visit them, and the picture of Toby faded a little from Muriel's mind with the compelling personality of his cousin. She could not help being aware of the flattery of being openly courted by a man who had half the county to choose from, and she knew as well as her mother did that while the vegetables and the strawberries might be intended for the widow's table, the roses were for her alone.

Mr. Brett's agent had just left him one day when the afternoon post was brought to him, with a packet in it addressed to "Stephen Ralston Brett, Esquire," in a handwriting that filled him with dismay.

Effie!...How dare she write to him here, at the Place? He opened the packet and found that it was a copy of *The Times*, neatly rolled up, and as he turned the pages he saw a cross marked against the casualty lists from South Africa. Some words were written in ink in the margin: "Don't forget that I am waiting for a telegram. Effie."

Stephen swore roundly, and was about to hurl the paper into the waste-paper basket when he remembered the housemaids' curiosity. There was no fire in the grate with which to destroy it, but there was a cupboard where a number of old photograph albums were stored, and he thrust it down at the back of them, intending to get it out and burn it at the first opportunity.

The threat contained in the newspaper dwelt with him so uncomfortably that he felt forced to forgo the visit to Ivy Lodge that had become almost a habit with him for that afternoon. He felt that Mrs. Lestrange would see that something was amiss, and he did not wish to bring a breath of a sordid past into the same house with Muriel.

He decided to ignore Effie's threats, and calling Toby's old spaniel, Beauty, he took her off for a long walk over the fields. Beauty, however, was getting fat and lazy in her old age and she dawdled, so that he had to stop and wait impatiently for her to catch up, frowning at the dark thoughts that kept pace with him.

There had been a time, long ago, when Effie had fascinated him. It had pleased his conceit to win her from Ricketts, and she had not been unwilling to play the beggar-maid to his King Cophetua. She was like a child in her delight over the gifts he heaped upon her, and was enchanted with the house, its pretty furniture, and its garden, and naïvely over-awed by her servants. They frightened her, she said laughing, because they knew so much more than she did.

She lived to please him in those days, and to delight him with her gaiety and her laughter, and her happiness seemed to depend upon his. It was only after the children were born that she had developed into a young woman who became more sure of herself with every day that passed, with a decided will of her own into the bargain, until Stephen had felt the iron bands of domesticity closing in about him.

Feeling stifled and resentful he had tried to break free with trips to the Continent, and a return to the bachelor life in the chambers that his father had before him. It was extraordinary, he thought now, viciously slicing off a delicate head of wild parsley with his cane, how possessive Effie had become. During the last year or two she might have been some suburban wife, questioning her husband as to where he had been, and what he had done, and the women he had met while he was away from her. It was long past the time to put an end to the affair, and he would put an end to it, come what may.

All that nonsense about sailing for South Africa had made him look a fool, as she had intended it should, and he would do no more beyond the settlement fixed by Fanshawe. She could do her worst.

Having thus settled matters in his mind he turned and whistled the spaniel to heel, making his way back through the lanes, and felt very sure of himself until he came within sight of the Place again on the far side of the park, and saw the wide sweep of the drive in front of it, and the pillared porch. And in that moment he found he could easily imagine that empty sweep filled by the station cab, bringing in it an over-dressed little woman, two children and a governess, and his heart sank, and if Calverley Ricketts had known then the dismay that he felt it would have made up a little for the things he had endured at his hands in the past.

He walked on swiftly to the village and entered the dark little post office and asked for a telegraph form. The post mistress, Mrs. Snagge, was one of his tenants: she knew almost more about his family than he did himself, and she would be extremely interested in the sad news he was having to convey to a lady with his own middle name.

Bitterly he cursed Effie for having set him such a problem, and having set down the name and address, "Mrs. Ralston, 47 Willowbrook Road, St. John's Wood, London," on the form, he was still staring at it not knowing how to proceed, when the shop door opened and Muriel came in for a dozen penny stamps.

She was surprised to find him there and greeted him coolly, aware of the post mistress at her elbow, but her eyes were kind and he took heart.

"I have to send a telegram to the wife of a relative of mine, telling her that her husband has been killed in South Africa," he said. "And I cannot think how to word it."

"I should think not indeed!" She was shocked. "But why should such a duty fall to you, Mr. Brett?"

"Unfortunately the War Office sent the notification of his death to me," he said. It was extraordinary how glibly the lies came once they were started. "I can only suppose that the poor chap's papers were lost and they could not trace his widow."

"I am so sorry for you." Muriel's voice was full of sympathy. "And for her, too, poor soul."

"What can I say to her?" He appealed to her boldly.

After thinking it over she said gently: "I should tell her the truth."

That startled him considerably. "The...truth?" he repeated uncertainly.

"I'm sure it would be kinder in the end. You could say, 'Have heard from the War Office of your husband's death'...No, that might be too harsh. I think I would say, 'Deeply regret to inform you that the War Office has notified me of your husband's death...'"

He began to write the words under the address, and then broke off in some confusion as she asked if the poor widow had any children.

"Two, I believe," he said, embarrassed, and she apologised for her curiosity.

"My mother was left in similar circumstances, you see," she told him. "And it has given me a fellow feeling for the poor lady. Are the children very young?"

"I'm not sure of their ages...but I shall instruct my solicitors to see that they don't want for anything, of course."

"How kind you are!" She turned to him impulsively.

"So kind and generous..." She broke off, confused by the look in his eyes. "I will leave you to finish it in peace," she said and bought her stamps.

He sent off the telegram and joined her outside, pleased to see that she was wearing one of his roses in her belt.

"They were so lovely," she told him. "I couldn't resist stealing one from the basket you sent Mother this morning."

"But they were for you," he said. "Surely you guessed that?"

Mrs. Snagge told the postman about the telegram. "Mr. Brett said it was a relative," she said. "But I don't recall there being any other Ralstons alive time Miss Emma Ralston married his father nearly forty years ago. I was a little gal then, and it were all the talk as Miss Emma were a lady of fortune with no living relatives, and that is why Mr. Stephen has always had money of his own, long before he come into the Place." She added thoughtfully, "Miss Lestrange was in buying stamps. I reckon she'll make a go of it with him. Kept watching her all the time, he did, and she was blushing and flashing her eyes at him under her big hat."

"Mrs. Lestrange's Eliza tells me he's allus in there for a bite to eat," said the postman with a grin. "One day it's tea, next it's luncheon or summat...Miss Lestrange will be mistress of the Place all right, you see if she won't, like she would be had Mr. Toby lived, poor lad."

"Mebbe he's well out of it then, if she only had her eye on the Place," said Mrs. Snagge sourly. "Whenever I see this Mr. Brett come into my shop I mind young Mr. Toby, last time he come in for a packet of postcards. Never had no change, hadn't Mr. Toby.... He'd give me half a sovereign and take a few bags of sweets for the village children instead. And didn't they know it, too? The young varmints would be waiting for him as he come over the green."

5

The telegram arrived in Willowbrook Road that evening, and on Miss Childs' advice Effie kept the news it contained from the children until the next day.

She did her best to exhibit some of the grief expected of her under the circumstances, but it was a considerable strain on her acting ability, and by the following morning she had recovered sufficiently to send a note by the boy to her dressmaker, ordering the best and most expensive mourning for them all, to be charged up to Mr. Fanshawe.

Having got this off her mind she sent for the children and found it more difficult than she had imagined to break the news to them. She began in a roundabout way by saying that they had to be brave and that their father was not coming back, but it was Kitty who guessed what she was trying to say and screamed out that he was dead. And in the midst of her anger with Stephen for having got her into such a situation once more Effie felt impatience with her daughter for not having Johnnie's more stolid acceptance of life.

In time Kitty recovered and for the rest of the day the children crept about on tiptoe, as if, their mother thought, Stephen's body was lying in the spare bedroom, and Miss Childs vetoed lessons for the day and took them into the garden to read to them there. The book she selected was *The Water Babies*, and Dalling the gardener was mowing the lawn, and for years afterwards the smell of mown grass would bring back to Kitty the sadness of *The Water Babies* and her first introduction to grief.

Her mourning order having been completed, Effie clothed herself and the children in black from head to foot, and wrote the promised letter to Mr. Fanshawe, and then she began packing up for the move, and Kitty's grief was softened a little by the thought of living in White Cliff Bay.

In due course the curtains were taken down from the windows of Number 47 Willowbrook Road, and in the first week in August while city dwellers were pouring out of London for the seaside, a steam engine harnessed to a furniture van arrived, and men in green baize aprons packed up the asparagus fern and its brass jardiniere, the drawing-room furniture, the carpets, the schoolroom piano, the oilcloth in the hall and the Rosalind portrait of Effie that Miss Childs had so much deplored. By some mischance, when other portraits were removed from the walls the only existing photograph of the late Mr. Ralston disappeared, and did not come to light again until the last of the bedroom furniture was being brought downstairs.

Sidney had come over from his parents' cottage in the Vale of Health to say goodbye, and he was sent out into the garden with Kitty to find the family cat, Tibs, who had vanished directly he saw the hamper open and ready to receive him on the kitchen floor. They came upon him in the empty toolshed, and Kitty picked him up in triumph and was returning with him in her arms, assuring him that he would not mind the journey nearly as much as he thought he would, when they passed the bonfire, and there, thrown carelessly down on a heap of rubbish still unburnt, was the photograph of the late Mr. Ralston, complete with its frame.

Kitty thrust Tibs into Sidney's reluctant arms and snatched up the photograph, and while he took the cat to Cook to be battened down in the hamper, she raced up the stairs to where Effie was seeing the last bit of her wardrobe out of her bedroom. It was a large one and there were six pieces altogether.

"Look, Mother!" Kitty flourished her find. "We nearly left this behind! It had been thrown on the bonfire by mistake but it's only a tiny bit scorched. Shall I give it to the men to pack?"

"If you give it to me, Missie," said one of the men good-naturedly, "I'll put it in one of these drawers."

"Certainly not! Those drawers are full of clothes." Effie's quick temper got the better of her. She took Kitty's hand in a firm grip and dragged her down two flights of stairs to the empty hall, where she swung her round angrily, her eyes blazing. "You naughty little girl!" she scolded her daughter. "To go picking up dirty old things from the bonfire. Look how you have marked your new black dress! Go and put it back at once!"

And then as Kitty stared at her, bewildered and frightened, Sidney appeared from the basement stairs. "I'll take it," he said quietly. He released the photograph from Kitty's paralysed hand and went away with it to the garden, and when he came back he found her alone in the drawing-room, sitting on the bare floor and weeping.

"Don't cry, Sugar Mouse!" Awkwardly he knelt beside her, putting a clumsy arm round her shoulders. "You'll melt away if you go on like that.... Look, Kit, your mother didn't mean to be unkind. She's worried about the move and there's a lot on her mind...But I'll tell you what I'll do after you are gone. I'll keep that photograph safe for you, and the first time I come to see you in your new home I'll bring it with me in a brand new frame. But we won't say anything about it; it will be a secret between us, see?"

Kitty stopped crying and flung her arms round his

44

neck. "Oh, Sid, you are a dear!" she cried and she kissed him, much to his embarrassment. "I do love you, Sid... I love you much better than I love Mother!"

"If Miss Childs heard you say that she's say, 'That, my dear, is extravagant and quite untrue.' Of course you love your mother. All good children love their mothers!"

She stole an uncertain look at him to see if he were joking, and he gave her a rough hug and helped her to her feet.

"I think we'd better see how poor old Tibs is getting on," he said. "He was screaming his head off when I left him with Cook."

They went off together and Miss Childs, meeting them in the hall, thought it was time she spoke to Kitty about holding Sidney's hand. She was getting too old for such childish behaviour and boys like Sidney Burke needed no encouragement.

The van moved off and a four-wheeler appeared to take the family to the railway station. Effie said good-bye to the servants: she had engaged an old party by the name of Clara Bucklethorn to be her general servant at Flint House, with the help of a boy of fourteen, Ted Twiddle, the greengrocer's nephew.

Then she kissed Sidney and sent her love to his parents, and went down the steps for the last time, pathetically elegant in her new black clothes. The gardener helped her into the cab and took charge of the key to the house, the children were packed away in the cab with Miss Childs, and Tibs in his basket, vociferously expressing his disapproval of the whole affair.

Sidney waited with the boy and the scullery-maid to see the cab turn the corners of the road, and then, as his companions set out after it, the boy wheeling the girl's basket holdall on a cart borrowed from the builder in the High Street, he went back into the garden to fetch the photograph from the rubbish heap.

Simpson had left the day before to take a post in the country where men-servants were kept, and Cook was sitting by the open window in the kitchen with her trunk standing ready beside her, talking to the gardener while she waited for her brother-in-law to fetch her.

Sidney sat down disconsolately in the swing and thought that he was going to miss the young Ralstons and their pleasant garden. The voices of Cook and the gardener reached him through the open window, and he listened idly: neither of them saw him sitting there in the swing, and it was not likely that they would have lowered their voices if they had.

"I won't keep you long, Mr. Dalling," Cook said. "My brother-in-law ought to be here soon."

"I'm not in no 'urry," said the gardener, who was in a philosophical turn of mind that morning. "Queer thing life, isn't it? Here today and gone tomorrow, as they say. Who'd have ever thought Mr. Ralston would be one to join the Volunteers and get hisself killed like he did?"

"Can't say as *I* was surprised." Cook gave a sniff that was full of meaning. "I've seen it coming for a long time now."

"What do you mean, seen it coming?" Dalling was mystified and Cook smiled in a superior fashion, while from the swing Sidney studied her with interest.

"Do you mean to tell me you was taken in by all that playacting, Mr. Dalling?" asked Mrs. Tapper. "All that talk of Mr. Ralston going to South Africa...and then that telegram coming so quick, like it did? He never got as near to South Africa as Nine Elms Station, let alone Southampton!"

"You don't say?" He stared at her, open-mouthed, while from the swing Sidney stared, too. "But I took the telegram from the boy myself, Mrs. Tapper!"

"But did it come from the War Office? Can you tell me that, if you please?"

"Why no, I can't then, seeing as I didn't read it."

"Well, I did then. I got it out of the waste-paper basket where Missus had throwed it, and I saw it was handed in at a place called Cranston, near Norwich, and signed by somebody called Brett. But that didn't

46

surprise me either, because I thought he was cooling off some time ago, and I've known his name wasn't Ralston since before Easter." Here she caught sight of Sidney and dropped her voice, the whispered words traversed the garden like the hissing of a serpent.

"The last time I went up to London along of my brother-in-law and his wife Elsie, and a friend of theirs by the name of Bert—I never did catch his other name—we was walking down the Strand in the afternoon when I see the master with a lady on his arm, just stepping into a cab. He was supposed to be in Paris over Easter, as you may remember. Well, this here Bert touches his cap respectful like, and after the cab had taken him and the lady off in the direction of Trafalgar Square I asks him who was the swell. 'Oh,' says Bert, 'that's Mr. Stephen Ralston Brett, that is, and his sister, Mrs. Cartwright. I used to work for their uncle, the late Mr. Richard Brett, as a stable-lad, when he kept some racing stables near Newmarket in the old days.' 'Did you now?' I says. 'And is this Mr. Stephen Ralston Brett a married man?' 'What, him?' says Bert with a laugh. 'I should think not indeed. He likes a gay life, does Mr. Stephen, though I've heard he keeps a lady friend somewhere out your way. Or it may be Putney,' he says."

A shocked silence fell on the garden, dry under the July sun.

"Of course," the gardener said constrainedly, "the missus was on the stage once. We all know that."

"And no call to be ashamed of it either," said Cook stoutly. "She was one of the nicest ladies I ever cooked for and that's the truth, Mr. Dalling. Nothing ever locked up and the store cupboard there for me to go to all times of day and night. Not that some wouldn't have imposed on her for it, mind: there's some I've known would have robbed her up hill and down dale. I could have sent eggs by the score out of this 'ouse, and I could have sold butter by the pound, but it's not in me nature to rob them as trusts me, Mr. Dalling, and never has been."

There was a whistle at the garden gate and the

brother-in-law was there with his cart, and while he and Mr. Dalling were loading on to it Mrs. Tapper's packages—some of which contained groceries which she assured them she could not bear to leave behind for the mice—Sidney slipped out and made his way back to Hampstead on his bicycle.

The gardener locked up and a few minutes later Number 47 was empty, and for the time being without life, until a TO LET notice appeared in its drawing-room window and a new tenant moved in, to fill it with his furniture and his problems, his family and his servants. In the garden the forgotten swing, would remain for a time, hanging crookedly from its branch, until the rain and fogs of winter rotted the ropes, when it would be cut down and thrown on the bonfire, beside an old photograph frame, still unburnt.

In his little room under the eaves of the Hampstead cottage Sidney sat on his bed thinking over what he had heard, and coupling it with Effie's queer behaviour over the photograph.

He took it from his pocket and stared at it, and the haughty eyes of Mr. Ralston stared back at him as if demanding what the devil it had to do with him, and if he had not promised Kitty she should have the wretched thing, he would have torn it in pieces and thrown them into the Hampstead ponds.

6

Except that it was exposed on all sides to the bracing sea air, there was little to recommend Flint House as an attractive residence.

In place of a parade White Cliff Bay had only a strip of asphalt with a few shelters, no pier, because piers would not stand up to the rough seas, and no flower beds, because flowers wilted and died in the salty spray. At one end the grey Martello Tower sat squat and ugly under the white cliffs and at the other the old Sailors' Rest marked the beginning of the Harbour Road, and between that and the Harbour itself Flint House stood like a fortress. At the back it looked over waste ground where concert parties and circuses pitched their tents in the summer, and in front it was only separated from the sea by the road and a strip of shingly beach.

But by the time the furniture arrived and the glass and china had been unpacked, and curtains were up at the windows, it lost some of its bleakness. The elderly servant, Clara Bucklethorn, scrubbed the place through, familiar pictures appeared on the walls, and the strangeness of the new home began to wear off.

Johnnie was at an age when every new thing was a delight and he gladly exchanged the daily walk in Regent's Park for the beach and rock pools under the cliff, bringing back handfuls of shrimps for Clara to cook for tea.

The weeks passed and Miss Childs suggested that her employer should appear at church as a signal to the residents that she was ready for them to leave their cards. Effie was amused at the suggestion.

"It would be simpler," she pointed out, "if one inserted a notice in the local paper to the effect that Mrs. Ralston's curtains were up at Flint House, the best silver was out of its baize covers, and she would be ready to receive callers next Thursday afternoon." She laughed at her governess's shocked face.

"I know it may seem extraordinary to adhere to such customs," said Miss Childs, trying to hide her disapproval. "But society is limited in a small town and people like to discover if newcomers know how to behave."

If there was a barbed shaft concealed in this remark Effie had no wish to look for it. "I suppose I should conform to etiquette where I can," she conceded good-humouredly.

"I think that for the sake of the children you should." agreed Miss Childs, and was puzzled afresh by the look that was half-scorn and half-laughter in the widow's pretty eyes.

Effie went off to church the next Sunday morning, fully aware of the eyes that cast up the cost of her mourning, and sang the hymns with the clear assurance of a well-trained voice, a fact that was noted and gave rise to a rumour that the new tenant of Flint House had been an opera singer.

A few people called, however, a schoolmaster and his sister, by the name of Grant, the Vicar and his wife, and the lawyer's lady, Mrs. Webber. The more important among the residents, such as Colonel and Mrs.

Crampthorne of Hill Court, and Judge Trivett and his three daughters at The Rookery, and old Lady Winter at the Gables, held aloof, preferring to wait until they could hear more detailed accounts of the newcomer. Effie was content that it should be so: she had noted that Colonel Crampthorne had an eye for a pretty woman and she had encountered his type before.

In September she told Miss Childs that she had an invitation to stay with a friend in London, and she left the children with the governess, returning at the end of October looking a great deal better for her stay. Miss Childs in the meantime was beginning to be worried by the stand-offishness of the people in the place, and she shared the young Ralstons' pleasure when early in November Wallie Burke brought his wife and Sidney to visit them. Under the circumstances she felt that even Sidney would be better than nothing.

On Sunday afternoon while the children were on the beach with Sidney and the governess taking a well-earned rest in her room, the comedian asked Effie how she was getting on.

"Stephen has died a decent death and we hope he is buried for good where White Cliff Bay is concerned," he said. "But is his lawyer giving you enough to live on?"

Her smile told him nothing. "My allowance would be considered adequate, I suppose," she said lightly.

"But one does not have to look far to see that you are not nearly as well off as you were in Willowbrook Road, my dear."

"Oh, no. But I did not expect to be." She glanced affectionately at the big, genial man, with his kindly, worried face, but her eyes were guarded.

"Have you made any friends down here, Effie?" asked Maidie.

"Goodness, no. The only people who have welcomed us are the tradespeople, who know from experience that I pay my bills!"

"Then why..." Maidie broke off and Effie laughed.

"Why did I choose to live here? Well, Stephen would

51

not let me stay in Willowbrook Road, and this was the only place I could think of at the time."

A glance passed between the Burkes and then Wallie said abruptly: "Effie, did you know that Stephen was married?"

"Yes, it was in the English...I mean, in the papers." She corrected herself swiftly. "I forget the lady's name?"

"I don't remember it either, but I heard she was a young lady who was living with her mother in Cranston village, and that she was desperately poor," said Wallie.

"That was to be expected," Effie said coolly. "Stephen enjoys being generous to penniless young ladies, and as he is rolling in riches he loses nothing by it, does he?" She spoke bitterly and Maidie changed the subject.

"We also heard that Cal is opening in London next spring in *The Second Mrs. Tanqueray*," she said.

"That too I'd heard," Effie said. "He wanted me to come back to the stage and make my debut in it...as Paula."

"As Paula?" Maidie forgot Stephen and his new wife in her delight for her friend. "But Effie that is wonderful news. You will accept the offer of course?"

"I don't know." Effie smiled serenely at their astonished faces. "I haven't made up my mind yet. I'm not a Mrs. Patrick Campbell, Maidie!"

"But Cal has great faith in you as an actress, Effie, as we all have. You're not much over thirty and as pretty as a picture still." Maidie was persuasive. "You could come back to the stage tomorrow and be sure of a welcome."

"If I wanted to," agreed Effie.

"Is it the children that makes you hesitate?" asked Maidie anxiously. "Couldn't you leave them down here in charge of Miss Childs?"

"I'd have to I suppose. You can't drag children of Kitty's and Johnnie's ages about from one lot of stage lodgings to another. Some are alive with fleas...and

52

worse! You and Wallie know that as well as I do, Maidie!"

"Some of the big stage families have done it successfully all the same. The Terrys for example..."

"I daresay they have, but I couldn't. Cal wouldn't allow it. And I haven't set foot on the stage since Johnnie was born. I might be a failure in spite of all that Cal could do for me. And if it is so easy for an actress to move her family around with her, Maidie, my dear, why have you and Wallie kept on that cottage in Hampstead?"

Maidie laughed unwillingly and Wallie admitted that there was something in that. "We keep our cottage," he added, "because it's cheap and provides us with a roof over our heads when I'm 'resting' as the saying is."

"And that doesn't happen often!" cried Maidie proudly.

"I'm not saying that it does... yet. But I'm not getting any younger.... Mind you, Effie, I won't say what we'd have done if Sid had decided to follow in his old Dad's footsteps. I daresay we might have given up the cottage then. But he set his heart on being a doctor, and that means time to study for examinations and a settled home in which to do it. Next year we hope he will be a student at the London University, which means that although later on he may have to take lodgings near the college and the hospital, for quite a time yet he will be able to go to and fro as he has done to the City of London School."

"But my children have to be educated too!" said Effie. "And I can't imagine Miss Childs in stage lodgings!"

"Couldn't you send them to boarding school?" asked Maidie. "Oh, Effie, you'd be starting at the top with Cal behind you! There'd be no dreary trudging round the agents' offices, no unsatisfying understudies' parts, no tours in 'Number Threes.' Can't you think out some solution for the children and go back to Cal, Effie? You'll never get such a chance again."

"I dare say I won't." But Effie did not seem very concerned about it. "Just now, Maidie dear, there is rather a lot at stake. I can't say that I wouldn't like to send Johnnie to boarding school though, because I would. At nine years old he can't be tied to a woman's apron strings much longer. He's bubbling over with high spirits, and he needs other boys to fight. He's had one sparring match behind the wood-shed with Mr. Twiddle's nephew Ted. Mr. Twiddle didn't like it at all."

Maidie laughed.

"Is there a school here that he could go to?" she asked.

"Oh, yes. Mr. Grant has been angling for him to go as a weekly boarder to St. David's." Effie made a small grimace. "The poor children wear Eton suits on Sundays and parade to church with silk hats on their heads. Johnnie thinks they are awful."

"But I daresay it is a good school, if you can afford the fees. Is there another school for Kitty here—a little day school where she could go?"

"Not a day school, dear! It is considered most *infra dig* in White Cliff Bay to send your children daily to school! They must be boarders or nothing! Miss Grant runs a little school at the Laurels next door to St. David's, but the two are quite separate. The boys would scorn to have anything to do with what they call 'the kids' next door, and Miss Grant's is a boarding-school for the daughters of people who are in India and other far-flung parts of the Empire. She has several very elegant young ladies to help her to look after her little girls, but I doubt if any of them are capable of teaching Kitty."

"That is a pity, because although I like your dear old Miss Childs, I do feel she oozes sympathy, Effie, and Kitty looks as if she needs a tonic now—not a sedative any more."

It seemed as if Kitty had found a tonic in Sidney when the children came in a little while later: her face glowed and she was laughing and settled down happily to an uproarious game of "Happy Families" round the dining-room table after tea.

As they travelled home on Tuesday Maidie said pensively to her husband: "I am surprised that Effie did not jump at Cal's offer, Wallie."

"Are you, my dear?" He watched the flying landscape out of the window for a moment and then he said, "Effie is rather a dark horse—always has been."

"Do you think she has some purpose of her own for living down there in the back of beyond?"

"She may have. I'd like to know where she went last month."

"She said she was staying with Lady Faulkner."

"I know she said that, and I was sorry to hear it, because that woman has a bad influence over Effie. She's not a very savoury character, Maidie, love."

"No, I suppose she isn't. But if Effie was not with her, where do you think she went?"

"Well, she made a slip when she said she had seen Stephen's wedding in the English papers—though she was quick to correct it. Didn't you notice it?"

"But...do you think she went abroad then?"

Wallie smiled. "I only know that Cal has been in Paris lately, fixing up a season there for his company."

"Cal!...Of course, that would account for it!"

"Account for what?"

"Why, for those lovely dresses in her wardrobe." Maidie glanced at Sidney in the opposite corner, deep in a book on biology and dropped her voice. "I saw them by accident when I went to her room last night to say goodnight. 'Why, Effie,' I said, 'what lovely new gowns! Did Lady Faulkner give them to you?' And she shut the wardrobe door quickly and said they were old dresses she had been having done up for when she was out of mourning. But I'd never seen them before."

"I can't see Cal having a great deal to spare for Effie, all the same. Not with that company of his to finance."

"Well, I don't think she is getting much from Stephen," Maidie said. "Poor Effie! I could cry when I think of her lovely house in Willowbrook Road. I'd be surprised if her household bills are more than three pounds a week in White Cliff Bay. On top of that I know she

55

has coal to find and wages to pay, but Miss Childs has never had more than twenty-five pounds a year and I should say old Clara would not ask more than eighteen." She paused and added resentfully, "With all his faults, I never thought that Stephen Brett was mean!"

"No," said Wallie decidedly. "Oh, no...Stephen is not mean." And then Sidney came out of his book and they began to talk of something else.

When Effie mentioned boarding schools to Miss Childs she was surprised to find that she raised no objection. The poor lady's dislike for White Cliff Bay was growing with the onset of winter, and she was no longer happy there, suspecting her favourite, Kitty, of having deceived her. She was positive that Sidney had given her some present that he did not want her to see, and yet when she taxed Kitty with it she flatly denied it.

"But I saw him take a parcel from his pocket and give it to you, dear," Miss Childs told her reproachfully. "Was it a book that you are not allowed to read? I won't be angry if you tell me the truth."

"It was not a book," said Kitty obstinately. "And it wasn't a present. It was something I'd left behind in Willowbrook Road."

Miss Childs did not believe her, but she reflected that when she had spoken to Mrs. Ralston once on the subject of her daughter's reading matter she had been told carelessly that anything immoral in a book would doubtless pass over the child's head, and so she said no more.

Mr. Grant agreed to take Johnnie as a weekly boarder after Christmas, but Kitty presented a more difficult problem as Miss Grant's pupils were much younger. After some hesitation, however, she said she would like to see some of her work.

"There is another girl of her age who has come to live here for a time with her grandmother, the dowager Lady Winter," she explained. "Her governess left to get married, and Lady Winter asked me to take Meg for a few lessons every day. Although I never take day

56

pupils as a rule I felt I might stretch a point for Lady Winter's grand-daughter."

"But of course!" said Effie. Miss Grant looked at her sharply.

"If Kitty is doing similar work I could take her for the spring term," she said coldly. "And possibly for the summer, too, if Lady Winter has no objection. But it will depend on how long Meg is to be here. I am afraid you will have to make other arrangements after July."

Effie understood the situation perfectly. To earn Lady Winter's recommendation to her friends was one thing, but to take unknown little Kitty Ralston except as a companion for Meg, was another matter altogether. She arranged for Miss Grant to come and have a chat with Miss Childs at half-past eight that evening, and Miss Grant told her brother later that the governess was no fool.

"She was full of the late Mr. Ralston's praises," she said. "She told me that he came from a very good family, and although he was in trade—a wine merchant, Edwin!—she thought he was put into the business by his family because of his marriage."

"His marriage, my dear?" Mr. Grant was puzzled.

"Yes, Edwin. Mrs. Ralston may have an amusing way of rattling on at one, and no doubt some men might find her attractive, though one cannot help feeling that a less exuberant manner would suit her better—having been so recently widowed. But Miss Childs says that she was not an opera singer, as we thought, but an actress! And we all know what *that* means!"

"Do we?" said her brother.

"Now Edwin, don't be tiresome! You know I have to be careful with little Meg Winter coming here."

"But Meg is staying with her grandmother simply because her brother was ordered sea air after his serious illness in the summer and their parents are to be in Athens until next autumn. Sir Arthur and Lady Winter are not likely to foster any childish friendships their daughter may make in your little school."

Miss Grant admitted the truth of this. "Miss Childs

says that Mr. Ralston did not visit them very often when they were in Willowbrook Road. She thinks the poor man regretted his marriage very much."

"Did he not live with his wife then?"

"Well, naturally you could not expect us to discuss that, Edwin!" Miss Grant was shocked by the bluntness of the question. "But his business seemed to take him away from home a great deal."

"Ah, yes...the wine business." Mr. Grant looked thoughtful. "Well, the boy is alert enough, and Kitty is an inoffensive little girl. I should say that her lesson-books are neater than Meg's: it should be a pleasure for you to teach her, and very good for little Miss Winter to have a girl of her own age to keep her company in her lessons."

The dowager raised no objection: she had seen Kitty in church, she remarked, and she did not fidget once during the Vicar's half-hour sermon, which was more than could be said for her grand-daughter.

And so in the New Year Miss Childs departed in the station cab with her luggage strapped to the roof, and although Kitty shed a few tears to see her go, the new and exciting world of school that awaited her softened the parting. And by the time Miss Childs wrote to her old pupil to give her her new address, the magic of the Winters had closed in about her, and she had forgotten her old governess completely.

7

As the weeks passed Kitty began to live for the hours when she could be with Meg. The dowager invited her to tea with her grand-daughter and approved of her enough when she came to allow her to play with Meg on the empty beach in the afternoons, where, on a Saturday, Johnnie sometimes consented to be their companion, honoured by the notice occasionally paid him by seventeen-year-old Bob Winter, who accompanied his sister as watch dog. But a nice watch dog, Kitty thought, and she was glad when Johnnie's chatter took the sad, withdrawn look away from Bob's handsome face.

There seemed to be little that her young brother had not learned about the sea-shore since they came: the different varieties of shells and sea-weed, the birds from the north that migrated in the winter to the warm beach under the cliff, the gulls that nested in the cliff-face, the fish that were caught by the fishermen and brought to the parade in the mornings to be sorted and sold down by the Martello Tower. Bob listened to it all with an air of amused astonishment that one small boy could assimilate so much knowledge in so short a time.

When the Easter holidays came Meg and Kitty were inseparable. Every fine day would see them on the beach, and if it should be raining the dowager's carriage would fetch Kitty for the day, bringing her back to Flint House in the evening.

But Lady Winter still did not call on Mrs. Ralston, and neither were her grand-children allowed to have tea at Flint House. The old lady told her friends that Kitty was an affectionate little creature and useful at keeping Meg amused, and in playing cribbage with herself, for which Meg had no patience, but it was tacitly understood that she would allow the acquaintance to develop no further. Naturally all this was talked over in the town and came back to Effie's ears, but she only laughed and held her tongue. The dowager might not find it as easy as she imagined, she thought, to drop little Kitty Ralston when the time came. And in the meantime Colonel Crampthorne often took his morning constitutional in the direction of Flint House.

During the Easter holidays Sidney came to stay for a few days, and Kitty could scarcely wait to introduce him to Meg, although when they met on the beach on the following morning she was chagrined to discover that Bob had nothing to say to him, although they were much the same age.

Meg made up for her brother's aloofness. After a moment's silence while Kitty tried desperately to find something to say that would gain Bob's respect for her friend, she observed: "So you are the great Sidney Burke! We've heard a lot about you, but Kitty didn't say what blue eyes you've got. I've never seen eyes quite as blue as yours, have you, Bob?"

The spell was broken and they laughed, while Sid coloured to his ears.

"I was taught that it was rude to make personal remarks," he said, the eyes in question meeting hers boldly.

"Oh, I was taught that too," said Meg airily. "But

I never pay attention to such things. I say what I like, and I expect I always shall."

"Meg," said Bob heavily. "Shut up!"

She made a face at him. "No then, I won't. I want to talk to Kitty's friend, and I don't see why I shouldn't." She smiled at Sidney rapturously. "Have you ever seen such a dull place as White Cliff Bay? Not even a pier . . . and only that silly old Martello Tower to go and stare at. Bob says it was built to defend the place against Napoleon, but I can't see it doing much good, can you?"

"Not in these days of ironclads, perhaps," Bob said, while Sidney's blue eyes regarded his sister with far more interest than he displayed in the Martello Tower. "But when there were only wooden ships, depending on sail and wind and tide, the guns from that tower would be able to blow them out of the water without much trouble."

"From what I've seen of the town," Sidney said, "I doubt if any of the inhabitants have heard yet that Napoleon is dead."

"You aren't to say such things about my dear White Cliff Bay!" Kitty was indignant. "I won't have it laughed at, and that old tower must have been very well built to stand up to all the gales that have battered it since it was put there."

"Very well I won't laugh at it," said Sidney. "Shall we go and have a closer look at it?"

"Oh, yes, let's!" Meg scrambled to her feet. "We'll leave Kitty here to keep Bob company, and he can go on with his history lesson. Kitty's fond of history and I'm not!" And off she ran, her feet so light on the shifting shingle that she was running along the broken asphalt long before he had reached it. But he was quick to follow, and went as willingly, Kitty noticed, as if he had not seen the old grey tower a hundred times before.

"I'm sorry!" Bob apologised for his sister. "Meg is a spoilt brat. It was unpardonable of her to take possession of your friend like that."

"I don't mind," Kitty assured him, not quite truthfully.

"But of course you mind!" he said sharply. "And so do I. I don't like such behaviour in my sister, and I'm sorry for Meg's friends. She uses them simply as a butt for her own cleverness in front of other people. She should know better."

Once again she felt her heart warming towards this delicate, handsome boy. He was so nice and friendly, and although his eyes might not be a brilliant blue like Sid's, they were comfortingly steady and direct. "I don't think I know what you mean?" she said shyly.

He smiled down at her thoughtfully. "Well, shall I say that she puts on an act...like a clown in a circus? Her friends have to be the stupid ones, so that she can say the things that get people laughing at her for being so witty, and at them for being fools...That's Meg."

"I hadn't noticed it," said Kitty perplexed.

"That's because you are naturally kind-hearted, while Meg is not at all. On the surface she is sweet and friendly but there is only one person she really cares for, and that is Margaret Winter. I am her brother, you see, and I know her as well as I love her."

"But I love her too, and I don't believe you know her at all."

He laughed. "If it makes you happy to believe that, don't let me destroy your illusions!" But when his sister came back, chattering away to Sid as if she had known him all her life, he took her firmly by the arm and marched her home.

"I'm sorry we have to leave so early," he said. "But Grandmamma is having friends in to lunch."

"That's the first I've heard of it," pouted Meg. "What friends? I don't know of any..."

"But then you don't know everything, my dear!" And Bob removed her from the scene with speed. Even so she waved her free hand to Sidney as she went.

"We shall be on the beach this afternoon!" she cried. "I will look for you, so mind you are there!"

But there was no sign of her or her brother on the

beach later on, and Kitty had to make excuses for them to Sidney, although she had the feeling that he was not listening.

"She's pretty, isn't she?" he said unexpectedly. "And she's fun, too. It's a pity her brother is such a stick."

"He isn't a stick...he's a dear," Kitty defended Bob quickly. "If he seems dull it's because he's been terribly ill and has to sit about a lot and read instead of playing games." But she thought that Sidney had taken a dislike to Bob and she was cross because his eyes danced at her excuses.

The next day the young Winters were not on the beach either, and Kitty began to have the uneasy suspicion that Bob was keeping his sister away from the Ralstons as long as their friend was staying at Flint House, and this became a certainty when Meg joined her on the beach on the morning after he had gone back to London.

"I suppose Sidney had gone?" she said in a vexed tone.

"Yes. He was only with us for a few days."

"I wanted to see him again," complained Meg. "He's so different from Bob's stupid friends. But Bob was so stuffy about him: I can't think why I have to have a brother. He's far worse than a governess and Grandmamma gives in to him, too. She says she has great faith in his judgement!"

Kitty tried to smile. "Didn't Bob like Sidney?" she asked.

"No, he didn't!" Meg made a face. "He said he was common!" And as her brother came down to the beach to them she repeated the accusation. "You did say Sidney Burke was common, didn't you, Bob dear?"

"He was the Ralstons' friend, not ours," said Bob quietly, with a wrathful look at his sister. "I did not want you to monopolise him for the whole of his visit."

Kitty felt that she should be grateful to Bob for his interference, but she remembered how Sidney had looked for Meg every day, and she felt that she had been a poor substitute.

Here, however, Johnnie put in unexpectedly, "Miss Childs said that Sid was common, too."

"She appears to be a lady of perspicacity," growled Bob, still too angry with Meg to choose his words, and Johnnie stared up at him with round eyes. "What does perspicacity mean?" he asked.

Nobody enlightened him, and Meg said airily: "*I* don't think Sidney's common, and if he is I expect it's because his parents are common, too. He said his father was 'on the halls,' and when I said I wasn't allowed to go to music halls he said he should think not indeed, so that shows that he knows what his father is like." She laughed and Kitty saw Bob's eyes resting on her gravely as if he expected her to defend her friends, but weak and cowardly as she knew herself to be, she could only laugh uncomfortably with Meg.

Not so with Johnnie. He stared at Bob stolidly and said loudly and clearly: "Well, I don't care what anybody says or thinks about Sid and Uncle Wallie and Aunt Maidie. They're my friends as much as they are Kitty's, and I like them, and I don't care if they are common or uncommon. They're jolly nice, all of them, and if anybody says a word against them I'll hit him on the nose, if he's twice my size. So there!" He doubled his fists and glared up at Meg's brother.

"Well, done, Johnnie!" Bob said quietly. "And I apologise if I appeared to pass judgement on your friends. Meg had no right to repeat what I said to her in confidence, and I didn't keep her away from Sidney Burke because I thought he was common, or anything like that. What he may or may not be is not my business, but I was not going to have his visit to you spoilt by my selfish little sister."

"Oh!" Johnnie looked relieved and his fists fell to his sides. "In that case, I expect it's all right then."

Bob held out his hand and they shook hands gravely and then Johnnie ran off to watch a fishing boat come in on the tide, to see what sort of a catch his friends the fishermen were going to land.

Bob sat down on the shingle, and taking a small

volume of Macaulay's Essays out of his pocket began to read.

"What *does* 'perspicacity' mean anyway?" asked Meg defiantly, angry with him for having snubbed her in front of her new friends. "I don't believe you know yourself, Bob."

He lifted his eyes briefly from his book. "It means the power to discern," he told her. "And it seems that Miss Childs managed to pass on that power to at least one of her pupils."

Kitty had the uncomfortable feeling that he did not mean her, because the glance he gave her was oddly reproachful, and she was glad that he returned at once to his book, leaving them to join Johnnie in watching the glittering, flashing wriggling mass of the netted fish.

That May the South African War ended and in June the sudden illness of the King meant the postponement of the Coronation and as a result of that, the postponement too of Sir Arthur and Lady Winter's return from Athens. All these events meant little to Effie, whose thoughts had been occupied lately with the urgent problem of her daughter's education.

It did not take her long to discover the name of the boarding school in Hampstead to which Meg was going that autumn, and one day in July she left Kitty in the charge of old Clara and went up to London and called on Miss Westlake, the Principal of the school. She found her to be a delightful woman, who agreed without hesitation to take Kitty when she knew that she was a friend of little Meg Winter, and although the fees in the prospectus made Effie gasp a little they did not make her alter her mind. Neither did Maidie's protests when she talked it over with her: she was staying the night with her friend in the Vale of Health.

"Of course I know the school by reputation," Maidie said doubtfully. "But the pupils are all very well-to-do, and come from the first families in the land."

"So much the better, and I am not paying the fees, dear! Mr. Fanshawe will do that."

"It isn't so much the fees as the girls themselves," Maidie pointed out. "Will Kitty be happy there, when they come from such a very different kind of life to her own?"

"If she is clever she will make it her life, too," said Effie. "They will have brothers, I suppose, who might be attracted to her when she is older?" She laughed suddenly. "I'd like to see old Lady Winter's face when she finds out that I am sending Kitty to Meg's school. It will be a proper score off the ill-mannered old creature!"

"But not at the expense of the child!" Maidie's soft heart misgave her. "Effie, don't you see how miserable she might be there?"

"If she is miserable it will be to spite me," said Effie shortly. "And if I know Kitty she will be in her seventh heaven when she knows she is not going to be parted from her beloved Meg."

On her way home she visited Peter Robinson's and ordered all the things that Kitty would need, from a hockey skirt to six pairs of woollen combinations, and having imparted the news to her daughter on her return to Flint House, endured her raptures with coolness and told her to make the most of her chances, which Kitty fervently promised she would, construing the word "chances" to mean education.

Although it was nothing to do with her, Miss Grant felt bound to apologise to Lady Winter's daughter-in-law when she arrived later in the month for the postponed Coronation, because of Mrs. Ralston's choice of a school for Kitty.

The younger Lady Winter opened her sleepy eyes wide.

"But I think it is an excellent thing for Meg to have a friend at the new school," she said and added, to Miss Grant's further astonishment, that she has called on Mrs. Ralston the day before and found her to be a pleasant sort of woman. Lethargic by nature and content to

66

take people as they came, Ursula Winter was always ready to drift into an acquaintance and to drift out of it as easily when it threatened to bore her, and she could not see why such an excellent practice should not extend to her daughter. "I have promised Meg that she shall come home every Sunday," she went on. "Our old coachman would make a terrible fuss if I wanted him to drive me anywhere on a Sunday, but he will make no trouble at all of fetching Meg from Hampstead to Belgrave Square and back again! I told Mrs. Ralston that I hoped Kitty would come with her." She added with her pretty laugh, "Meg adores her and has made the poor child her slave, and even my mother-in-law says she plays cribbage quite excellently for her age."

"Ah, yes, but then I feel that Kitty must take after her poor father." Miss Grant felt bound to put in a word for the late Mr. Ralston.

"I must say I liked Mrs. Ralston." Lady Winter got up to go. "Like most actresses she is pretty and vivacious, but under it all I should say she has a great deal of shrewd common-sense." And then she thanked Miss Grant for the trouble she had taken over Meg's lessons, said that she hoped they would meet again someday, and was driven away in the dowager's carriage.

"Meg's mother seems to have taken a fancy to Mrs. Ralston," Miss Grant told her brother acidly that evening. "I should not have thought they would have much in common."

"Lady Winter is very charming," Mr. Grant observed mildly. "I daresay she wanted to make amends for her mother-in-law's unfriendliness before Meg left White Cliff Bay."

"I wonder if she noticed that there are no photographs of Mr. Ralston at Flint House?" said Miss Grant spitefully. "It has always struck me as being extremely odd that although there are plenty of Mrs. Ralston and the children, there is not one of him."

"Perhaps he did not like being photographed, my dear. A number of men don't—myself for one."

Miss Grant said she had a headache and would go

to bed. She felt annoyed with Lady Winter and Edwin for refusing to be drawn into discussing Mrs. Ralston. "Nobody can say that I listen to gossip or pass it on," she complained. "I only hope that Lady Winter will not have cause to be sorry in the future that she has taken up little Kitty Ralston and her vulgar mother."

Kitty went off to school that September looking very grown up in her navy blue serge jacket and ankle-length skirt, with her hair tied back with a large black bow on the nape of her neck, and the regulation sailor hat with its navy-blue ribbon on her young head. She carried her hockey-stick and a small Gladstone bag with her night-things in it, while her new trunk, packed with new clothes, went on ahead of her.

She felt nothing but pleasureable excitement at the thought of the journey, in charge of the guard, and the prospect of seeing Meg again. In her trunk there travelled her father's photograph, in Sidney's smart new frame, smuggled in after her clothes were packed without Effie's knowledge.

"It shall have a place of honour on my dressing-table," thought Kitty. "I'm not going to hide it away there, whatever I may have to do with it at home. What a good thing it was that Sid saved it from the bonfire!"

Fortunately it was to be some years before circumstances forced her to change this opinion.

8

Kitty settled down happily in Miss Westlake's school and nearly every Sunday she went with Meg to the Winters' big house in Belgrave Square, which to her inexperienced eyes resembled a palace in its size and contents. It took her some time to overcome her awe of the butler, Grayson, and the superior manners of the tall footmen. Old Lady Winter had only women indoor servants at The Gables.

On the few occasions when she was invited to the Burkes' little house it seemed small and poor after the magnificence of Belgravia. Sidney had matriculated and was now a student at the London University, and when Kitty went to the Vale of Health he was never there, although she heard a lot about him from his proud parents, and about the red-haired sister of a friend of his who, according to Wallie, had quite "bowled him over." Wallie walked back with her to the school in the evenings, larger than ever in his checked suit, his overcoat with its imitation fur collar, his brown bowler hat and his yellow spats, and Kitty heard little of his conversation, so anxious was she that their arrival might not coincide with the appearance of Meg in her father's carriage.

Sir Arthur had returned to Athens directly after the Coronation, leaving his wife at home for a time. The doctors still would not pass Bob as being fit enough for the rough and tumble of school life, and so he had not returned to Harrow, but was studying with a London crammer to whose house he went daily from Belgrave Square.

Kitty's continued friendship with the Burkes became one of the things on which she and Meg quarrelled.

"I cannot see why you must go and see them instead of coming out with me on a Sunday," Meg complained. "You say that Sidney is never there, so why do you go? Have they got a nicer house than ours?"

"Of course not!" Kitty laughed. "It is only a tiny cottage, with a flower bed in front and a cabbage patch at the rear."

"It sounds like a workman's cottage!"

"It was a workman's cottage, until they went there."

"Will Sidney be there the next time you go?"

"I don't suppose so. He hasn't been there at all yet."

"Then I'd stop going to see them if I were you."

Kitty flushed. "I can't do that. It would hurt their feelings."

"Oh, *feelings!* ... What do they matter, when it's so dull and uninteresting for you? Next time Mrs. Burke asks you out you can say you've got a cold and can't go."

"But that wouldn't be true."

"What of it?" Meg laughed. "Doesn't your mother ever say she's not at home to tiresome callers? I know mine does!"

But Kitty was thinking of Johnnie's quick defence of their old friends, and the look on Bob's face when she had laughed at them with Meg, and she said quietly: "The Burkes ask me out because they think I might be homesick."

"Then they won't mind a bit if you don't go!" cried

Meg triumphantly, adding, "After all, you can always drop people when you don't want to be bothered with them any more, can't you?" She glanced at her with laughing malice. "But I don't suppose you really want to drop the Burkes because of Sidney, and I don't blame you for that. If Bob wasn't so silly I'd ask Mother to invite him out to lunch with us one Sunday, but he would never let anything as nice as that happen. While Father is abroad he thinks he is the master of the house. I wish he hadn't been so ill: he'd be back at Harrow now, instead of being at home, spoiling everything." She sighed impatiently. "It's stupid being a girl and not being allowed to choose one's friends. Why should all my friends be selected by my mother and my brother?" After a minute she added, "Look, Kitty, why don't *you* ask Bob if Sidney can come to lunch with us one Sunday? He might agree to it for you, because Sidney is your friend, you know!"

Kitty said that she did not think it likely.

"Oh, but Bob likes you," said Meg unexpectedly. "He thinks that you have a very good influence over me! Do try, Kitty! Just to please me!"

Kitty gave in unwillingly, and the next Sunday she followed Bob into the library after lunch and timidly put forward the request. His reply was disconcertingly final.

"No, Kitty, I'm afraid it is impossible." And then as she coloured up he added more kindly, "Meg put you up to this, didn't she? You needn't answer. I can usually recognise Meg's work when I see it. I'm not having a guest of ours used by my sister as an excuse for inviting every young bounder she fancies to the house." He broke off. "I'm sorry...I should not have said that."

Kitty looked at him with puzzled eyes. "What is a bounder, Bob?" she asked.

"Oh, Lord!" He gave a rueful smile. "How am I to explain that if you don't know?"

She was abashed, feeling that she should have known, and that in some odd way it was her fault because she didn't. "Is it the way Sidney speaks?" she asked. "Miss Childs said he has a Cockney accent, but he put it on a lot to tease her because he knew she disliked it."

"It's not altogether the way a fellow speaks, Kitty." Bob hesitated, trying to find words for what he felt about Sidney. "It's more the things he says...the way he behaves...the clothes he wears...Oh, it's impossible to describe really. A chap's either a gentleman or a bounder—he can't be both." He smiled at her. "You are still looking perplexed. I'm afraid I haven't succeeded in making it very clear. Don't worry your head with it any more, but run off and tell Meg that her plot is discovered."

She laughed with him, secretly relieved that he had squashed the project. She had no fear of Sidney's success with Lady Winter: she thought that Meg's mother would have liked him. But she thought that Grayson might not have approved of him at all, and the tall footmen would have had a lot to say in the servants' hall.

To please Meg, however, she asked Miss Westlake if she might refuse Maidie's next invitation, and she was disconcerted by the headmistress's reply. "Why don't you want to go?" she asked coldly.

"Well..." Kitty fidgeted. "I'd rather go out with Meg."

"I daresay you would. But Mrs. Burke is an old friend."

"Yes." Kitty's eyes met hers pleadingly. "But need I go just this once?"

Miss Westlake frowned. With her gold pince-nez, her dark hair plaited and twisted into a bun on top of her head, her stiff, frizzed fringe, and the high linen collar to her flannel blouse, she looked more severe than she really was.

"My dear little girl," she said gently, "I don't think your mother quite realised the type of pupil that my school attracts, when she sent you here. The girls come from wealthy families, and are accustomed to a way of living that, from what I know of your mother's circumstances, may not be possible for you. Think carefully therefore before you shelve old friends for new, because I warn you, my dear, that people who want you to 'drop' old friends in whom they have no interest will just as readily 'drop' you in your turn." She might have overheard her conversation with Meg, and Kitty coloured and remained guiltily silent.

Miss Westlake looked at the watch tucked into her belt and said that it was time for lessons to begin. "I will tell Mrs. Burke that you have a previous engagement for next Sunday," she added, "but if you are invited to her house again this term I'm afraid you must accept."

"Yes, Miss Westlake. Thank you." Kitty escaped to whisper the good news to Meg before the French lesson began, and was disappointed when her friend received it with only a qualified pleasure.

"I'm sure I don't want you to stop seeing your precious Burkes," she observed cruelly. "I can easily take Daisy Drayton out if you don't want to come."

Now Meg knew that if there was one girl that Kitty disliked it was the younger of the two Drayton sisters, a girl with a pallid unhealthy complexion marred by spots, fair mousy coloured hair, and a weak chin, but before she could reply Mademoiselle Gaudet rapped on her desk for silence and they had to get out their translation books.

There was an uneasy feeling of ingratitude in Kitty's heart however over her treatment of the Burkes, and all the time she was with Meg that Sunday she found her thoughts straying back to the little house in the Vale of Health, and she wished she had been brave enough to tell Meg to take both the Drayton girls with her if she wished. But she had learnt by now that Bob knew what he was saying when he tried to warn her against his sister, and that with her fickle nature Meg would be quite likely to take her at her word. And to be at school with Meg and find herself supplanted in her affections by the spotty, weak-chinned Daisy was quite unthinkable.

After the Christmas holidays Kitty heard a great deal about a handsome cousin of Meg's who had been spending Christmas with them in Belgrave Square.

"He passed out of Sandhurst a year ago," she said. "And now he's got a commission in his father's old regiment. He is such fun and so good-looking, and I wouldn't be surprised if he spends most of his leave with us now, because his sister has just married a man he detests and his mother is living in the same village. He said that while he was staying with Aunt Helen—that's his mother—in Cranston waiting for his commission to come though, his brother-in-law was quite odious to him, and he's given poor old Aunt Helen his awful old Dower House to live in because he wanted her nice little house for his sister. Richard says it is much too big for Aunt Helen and bitterly cold."

"He sounds a horrid man," said Kitty, polishing up the silver frame to her father's photograph with her best handkerchief.

"I wish you could meet Richard," Meg said insincerely. "But he's off to Ireland in February and after he's had a year or two there he is going to put in for his service in India." She went on with a touch of restraint, "Did you see your friend Sidney in the holidays? I expect he's forgotten all about me by now?"

"Indeed he hasn't," said Kitty warmly. "He was in Brighton with Aunt Maidie for a few days and they came to see us. He asked if you were as pretty as ever."

Meg flushed with pleasure. "And you said that I was quite hideous, I expect?"

"I said you were prettier," said Kitty simply.

"I *do* like your Sidney," Meg said.

At the end of the summer term that year Miss Westlake gave her annual concert, to which pupils were allowed to invite their parents and friends, and as Effie was not there Kitty was included in the Winters' party at the buffet supper afterwards. Bob had escorted his mother, but he seemed quieter than usual and Kitty tried to find something to say that would take the gravity from his eyes.

"Meg tells me you are going up to Oxford in the autumn?" she said at last. "It has all been settled then?"

"Yes." He brightened up. "The doctors have given me permission to go, on condition that I abstain from all forms of violent exercise—such as rowing and running and boxing, and all the things that undergraduates go in for! But if I am very good I may be permitted a game of cricket in my last year."

Kitty laughed. "I expect they are only being extra careful," she said and added. "I'm so glad you are well again now Bob, though Meg and I will miss you on Sundays."

"You'll have to solve your own problems now," he said smiling. "I san't be there to help you."

"Oh, you needn't think you will get off scot-free, because I shall send you my essays to correct. Nobody can write essays better than you do, Bob."

"When one is forbidden to use one's legs, one has to employ one's hands instead." He looked down at her affectionately. "I shall trust you in return to keep an eye on that incorrigible sister of mine, and see that she doesn't get into mischief while I am away."

"Meg isn't half as bad as you make her out to be," she protested. "A lot of it is just her nonsense, and she doesn't mean anything by it. She is so alive, so eager to live, and she gets impatient with being a schoolgirl still. She wants to have done with it and to be grown up, and it is very trying for her to be treated like a small child with no mind of her own."

His grey eyes studied her intently. "Does she say that I do that?" he asked.

"Well…yes. And there are times when you *do*, you know!"

"Perhaps I have been a bit severe," he agreed. "I keep forgetting that schoolgirls are romantic creatures, with their head stuffed full of dreams."

"I don't think mine is," she said seriously.

"But then I've noticed that yours is a very sensible

little head, Kitty. I wish Meg's were more like it. All the same, I suppose you want to grow up, too?"

"I don't know." She shot a troubled glance at him. "Have you ever felt that the present is good enough, and that if you are too impatient to look into the future there may be something that you won't like waiting there for you?"

"I may have felt it, but there has been a reason for that." His face was suddenly sad. "But for you there could be nothing to make you feel that way, surely?"

The sympathy and concern in his voice made her suddenly shy of him. "No of course not," she said quickly and was glad that the Draytons came over with their parents to interrupt their conversation.

That August when Sidney snatched a few days to come down as usual to Flint House Kitty found it difficult to talk to him about her new friends.

"I should say it will do Bob Winter a great deal of good to go up to Oxford," he commented. "Knock some sense into him. I only met him once, but that was enough. I can't bear these stuck-up fellows."

"Bob isn't stuck-up!" cried Kitty indignantly. "He's a gentle, nice person...and he's been so ill, Sid."

"What was the matter with him?"

"I'm not sure but I know it was very serious."

"More likely to be a slight illness exaggerated into a bad one because my lord didn't like school," Sid said brutally. "I'm sorry for that pretty sister of his."

The most popular beach in White Cliff Bay was near the Martello Tower, where there were small stretches of sand at low tide, but they were sitting on the shingle in front of Flint House, where the stones were like cobble-stones, and they had it to themselves. Kitty picked up a stone that had a crystal hole in it and rolled it gently from hand to hand so that the crystal caught the sunshine. She did not want to talk about Bob any more, and fortunately Sidney had other things beside Bob on his mind. He picked up a handful of stones and began to throw them with deliberation into the water, each a bit further out than the last, and presently he said carelessly. "By the way, Kitty, what happened to that photograph of your father? Have you still got it?"

"Why yes." She was surprised at the question. "Mother doesn't know, of course, but when I'm at school I keep it on my dressing-table beside the one of her and Johnnie."

"Do you think that's wise?"

"What do you mean?" She was so surprised that he did not reply for a moment. And then as the last of his stones fell short of the others he tried again.

"Well, you see, Sugar Mouse, I've been thinking since I gave that photograph to you that there might be some perfectly good reason why your mother did not want one of him in her house. It could be—and mind you this is pure surmise on my part!—that she did not want anybody to recognise him."

"But why shouldn't people recognise him?" And then she caught a glimpse of his face. "Sidney, you know something about my father! I'm sure you do!"

"No, I don't. Honest I don't! Cross my heart and hope to die..." Hastily he tried to reassure her. "But I've had attacks of conscience from time to time over the confounded thing. Your mother wanted it destroyed... and she must have had a reason for it."

She stopped playing with the stone in her lap; the crystal in it seemed to have gone dead. "Wait," she said slowly, "I think I see what is in your mind. You think that Father might have done something terrible—like robbing people who trusted him—and that is why Mother has no portrait of him?"

"I think nothing of the sort!" Yet how could he explain the truth to this absurdly innocent young creature? "Your father would never have done anything dishonourable—at least nothing that *his* world would have thought dishonourable," he added, more to himself than to her. "Has Meg ever remarked on the photograph? I think you said you shared a room with her?"

"She has only remarked how handsome he was. *Her* father is short and tubby and bald."

"Oh, well. I daresay it's all right then." He managed

77

to quieten his conscience: after all it was very unlikely that a member of Brett's family would come as a pupil to Miss Westlake's school. "Don't worry over it any more," he said, and taking the stone from her lap he threw it after the others and only when it had fallen with a splash into the deepest part of the water did she remember that he had thrown away the crystal, too.

Sidney did not stay long that year and Kitty wondered if it was because Meg was not there. He was not to meet Meg until two years later, as it happened, and those years were busy ones for them all, for Bob at Oxford, for Sidney in London, for the two girls in Hampstead, growing up fast, and for Effie, joining Calverley Ricketts in stolen meetings whenever she could and bringing with her large cheques from the children's money.

And then in the summer of 1905 Miss Westlake decided to replace the annual concert with an end of term ball, to which the girls might invite their brothers.

Maidie had invited Kitty out one Sunday towards the end of that term, and Sidney happened to be paying one of his rare visits home that day. He walked back with her over the Heath through the summer evening, wheeling his bicycle and talking about the second part of the Intermediate Examination in which he was secretly afraid that he had not done very well owing to an inclination to frivol with fellow students rather than get down to the business of hard work. He talked about himself as they went, because it did not occur to him that his companion would not share his own deep interest in his affairs.

As luck would have it they overtook Miss Westlake on her way back from evening service at Hampstead Parish Church, and she stopped to talk to Sidney and to admire his bicycle.

"I expect you ride out in the lanes round Finchley?" she said. "Or do you go further afield?"

He said he had little time for cycling because he had been busy with exams, and she was sympathetic at once, her woman's heart melting to his blue eyes.

"I can't think why I wanted to be a doctor," he complained. "I should have gone on the halls like my father."

"And why didn't you?" she asked smiling.

"Oh, I wouldn't have been any good at all. I can dance and sing a bit because the old man used to rehearse his new acts with me when I was a kid, and he was very particular that everything should be A.1 and copper bottom, if you know what I mean?"

"I know exactly what you mean." She laughed at his surprise. "Although I do not permit slang in my school, when I was young I had five brothers and my language was anything but pure at that time!" And then to Kitty's delight she went on. "But if you can dance, will you not come to our end of term ball? It is too far for Kitty's brother to come, but I am sure she will be pleased to send you an invitation in his place, won't you, Kitty?"

"Oh, yes! Thank you, Miss Westlake. *Do* come, Sid!" Kitty was so eager that he had not the heart to refuse, although a schoolgirl's dance was scarcely an entertainment to promise any great excitement. And then he mounted his bicycle and rode away, and directly she got back to the school Kitty raced upstairs to impart the good news to Meg.

Bob had gone for a month's holiday to Switzerland with a college friend, and his cousin, who was on leave from Ireland, came in his place, resplendent in mess uniform and handsome enough to turn all the girls' heads.

"Kitty," Meg said, "let me introduce my cousin, Richard Lestrange." And then in a lower voice, "Hasn't Sidney come yet?" Kitty shook her head and Meg gave a smothered laugh. "Shame on him for a coward! Though I must say I had the greatest difficulty in persuading Richard to face fifty girls all at once!"

And then there was a little stir in the doorway and a familiar voice was heard apologising for being late. "My front tyre sprang a puncture just as I was starting,

Miss Westlake," said Sidney. "And so I had to walk. I was scarcely dressed for mending punctures, you see!"

Across the room Kitty saw Sidney, so immaculate in his well-fitting dress suit that nobody would have guessed that he had borrowed it from a fellow student for the occasion, and at the same moment he saw her and came to her smiling. At seventeen, with her dark hair tied in its big black bow, and her dress the high-necked white party dress of a schoolgirl still, she did not look much more mature than the nice, serious child he had always known.

"Am I too late for the next dance?" he asked, but before she could reply Meg answered for her.

"Yes, you are, Mr. Burke. Much too late! She is dancing this with my cousin, aren't you, Kitty? But I have kept one for you, because she told me you were coming. I was afraid that you were going to make a wallflower of me because of my kind heart!"

If Kitty were not mature, the same could not be said of Meg. Her dress might have the high neck that was required, but the lace was so transparent that it might have been a low one after all. She had put up her hair for the dance too, "just to see what it looks like," she told Kitty, and the lovely face it framed held Sidney's eyes, and the many girls he had met and admired since he had last seen her faded from his mind.

From that moment the evening took on a dreamlike quality for Kitty. She remembered seeing Richard Lestrange smiling down at her and hearing him say, "It seems we are left with no choice, Miss Ralston! I only hope you will forgive my bad dancing, and blame Meg for it and not me!" before he swept her away into the waltz that was just starting.

Sidney was left to stare at Meg, bewitched by her sparkling beauty, her curling chestnut hair, and the eloquence of her hazel eyes.

"Perhaps you would rather have danced with Kitty?" she said demurely, with the suspicion of a pout.

"You know I wouldn't," he said in a low voice. "But you took my breath away." He put his arm round her waist and piloted her on to the floor of the big school-room that had been cleared for the dance.

"Poor little Kitty," she said. "I hope I wasn't unkind to her. But I did give her Richard in exchange, didn't I? Dear Richard dances like most hunting men—as if he were riding for a fall! I find it a little exhausting. I hope he won't tread on Kitty's toes too much. I'm *very* fond of Kitty, aren't you?"

"Kitty is a nice little Sugar Mouse," he said briefly.

"Is that what you call her?" She looked up innocently into his face. "But if she is a sugar mouse—what am I?"

"Oh, you..." he said and paused.

"Yes?" Her laugh was light and lovely. "I'm waiting, Mr. Burke!"

"You," he said gently, "are the eternal Eve, and I suspect that you know it, Meg!"

She did not say that she didn't. "Kitty says you are going to be a doctor," she said. "But you cannot possibly spend your life looking at people's horrid tongues and prescribing nasty pills, when you dance as divinely as this!"

"What do you advise me to do then?"

She gave him a slanting glance. Yes, she thought, she did like his eyes. In fact, she liked him altogether. In fact, she wouldn't be surprised if he was the sort of person one could almost fall in love with...."I know what you must do." she said gaily. "You must be a very famous and successful doctor. You must operate on the King...or get yourself appointed as physician to a Royal Household. There are plenty to choose from!" She broke off, blushing at the look in his eyes. "I don't know what it is about you that makes me talk nonsense, Mr. Burke. I did it when I first met you, didn't I? I'm afraid you must have a bad influence on me!"

"Nobody could dream of having any influence over you, Miss Winter. You are a law unto yourself, and you always will be, won't you?" Again their eyes met and Meg laughed.

"Well, maybe I will," she said, and then the dance

81

ended and he took her back to Kitty and Richard Lestrange.

Miss Westlake's summer ball was all that a summer ball should be, although it was danced with decorum under her indulgent eye. It contained sets of Lancers, a quadrille or two, a romping polka, some waltzes in which the girls revolved lightly in their partners' arms, and in which Meg and Sidney daringly attempted to reverse while Miss Westlake was not looking. It ended at midnight with Sir Roger de Coverley, after which the orchestra packed its instruments and went away into the star-lit night, and the girls drank cups of hot cocoa before saying goodnight to their partners and going upstairs to bed.

It was stupid, Kitty thought wistfully, to wish that Sidney had spared more dances for her, when he was enjoying dancing with Meg. But then Meg had so much to say to her partners and she had so little and there had been a grown-up assurance about Richard Lestrange that had made her shy and tongue-tied as she never was with Bob. But then Bob always understood what she wanted to say before she put it into words, as Sid used to do in the old days.

It was stupid to feel that Sid had been lost to her finally that evening: she should be glad that Meg liked him so much. It was nice, she told herself fiercely, seeing the moonlight on the window through a mist of tears, when one's friends took to each other like that. Only a very mean-minded person would feel envious because they had enjoyed themselves, and unhappy because Bob had not been there....

9

Richard walked down the empty street with Sidney towards a cabstand at the bottom, and as they strolled along in the soft, lovely night he said lightly: "Pretty little girl, that friend of Meg's. I understand that you have known her family for some time?"

"Yes," said Sidney, his mind bemused with Meg.

"What happened to Mr. Ralston?" asked Richard.

"What happened...? Oh, he was killed in South Africa." There had been a light in Meg's eyes when she said good night and a soft warmth in her voice when she said they would meet again, as if she had really believed it.

"What is Mrs. Ralston like?" asked Richard. "Is she pretty?"

"In a doll-like kind of way. Kitty's not a bit like her." Sidney dismissed the Ralstons impatiently, but it seemed that Richard had not finished with them yet. He was a young man who liked to sift things to the bottom, a trait that was already earning him a reputation in his regiment, the senior officers appreciating it as much as the ranks did not. He asked who Mrs. Ralston was before she married.

Sidney shrugged his shoulders. "She was on the stage," he said. "I'm afraid that is all I know about her." The line of gaslamps down the street were as pale and mysterious as the pearl ornament in Meg's hair.

"So that one might conclude, I suppose, that Mr. Ralston married beneath him?" pursued Richard.

Sidney frowned. "What of it?" he asked shortly.

"Well, it might make a difference to his daughter, if you see what I mean?"

"I am afraid I don't." They had reached a turning that led towards the Heath, and Sidney stood still, momentarily forgetting Meg and suddenly hostile.

"I don't mean anything derogatory, my dear fellow!" Richard took his arm in a friendly grasp. "Your little friend is charmingly pretty, even if her conversation is rather limited at present. But she will grow out of that when she is 'out' and has admirers round her by the score. The thing that interests me about her is her name—the name of Ralston. It is a very familiar one to me."

"Oh?" Sidney's air of resentment changed subtly. "In what way?"

"Because it is my dear brother-in-law's middle name, and I can't quite conquer an absurd notion that she may be related to him. She is rather like him to look at, but she seems to know nothing about her father's family."

Sidney did not reply and he went on lightly: "Stephen Ralston Brett is one of those pompous asses who can't see further than his own park railings, and his mother's family—the Ralstons—may have been like him in that respect. In which case a mésalliance would certainly upset them. But I detest the fellow and I would not like to think that little Miss Ralston were related to him for her own sake. It would not be a relationship to boast about."

"Stephen Ralston Brett is your brother-in-law?" asked Sidney in a slightly constrained tone.

"Yes. Have you met him?"

"No...Oh, no. Never met him in my life." To Sidney's relief a hansom overtook them at that moment on its way to the cabstand and Richard hailed it. Sidney said good night to his companion with a warm handshake and an inner hope that they would not meet again.

It was an odd chance, he mused, as he made his way home across the Heath, that had sent Richard Lestrange to Meg's school that night to dance with Stephen Brett's daughter, but army leave was intermittent and it was not likely that he would meet her again, any more than a medical student like himself would be likely to meet Sir Arthur Winter's daughter.

As the vivid memory of Meg came back he was able to dismiss Kitty from his mind: the sky over the Heath was a wide expanse of stars, twinkling and shining and stabbing into the night, as bright as a future that might still hold Meg, as bright as Meg's eyes, and even a medical student, he supposed could have his dreams.

When Meg angled for an invitation for her cousin to join her at her grandmother's house for a few days, Richard was quite agreeable, although he was a little surprised by her desire to go to The Gables.

"I thought you could not stand your Grandmamma's family prayers?" he said.

"Oh, I don't mind getting down by half-past eight in the summer," said Meg airily. "I'm not nearly as idle as you think I am."

Richard's furlough was short, but not too short for him to look forward to a few days of sailing and fishing, and the ugly little town was a great deal more inviting to him than Cranston, where his brother-in-law was preparing for his departure to Scotland for the Twelfth, there to vent his disappointment on the grouse rather than on his wife, because Muriel had just presented him with a fourth daughter instead of the son and heir he had confidently expected.

But when, on the morning after his arrival at The

Gables, Richard accompanied Meg to the beach and found there Sidney Burke with Kitty Ralston and her schoolboy brother, he guessed what had been going on in his cousin's mind, and later that morning, as he walked back with her to lunch, he accused her bitterly of duplicity.

"You knew all the time that fellow was to be here," he told her indignantly. "No wonder you were so anxious to come and see your darling grand-mamma. Such a display of devotion to the old lady was highly suspect, coming from you!"

"I don't know what you are fussing about, Rick. Mr. Burke only said that he might be staying down here for a few days with the Ralstons." Her face was demure but her eyes were dancing. Richard refused to smile.

"You knew quite well he would be here if you gave him the least hint that you would be at The Gables. The poor chap is badly smitten with your young charms, God help him, and you are just leading him on!"

"Don't be angry, darling Rick!" She insinuated her hand into his arm. "You sound like Bob. He always grudges me my little bits of fun, and it isn't kind when I have to be shut up in that awful school for weeks on end, like a—like a nun in a nunnery!"

"What may be fun for you might turn out to be the reverse for a chap like Burke," Richard pointed out. "You know you will drop him like a hot cake the moment somebody more amusing comes along. You are a graceless minx, Meg."

"Am I?" She looked pleased. "Do you know, Rick, I think I'll ask Mother if I can have Kitty to stay for a week in London when we have our New Year's dance? She would enjoy it so much, poor darling. I don't think the Ralstons know anybody down here, and it must be so dull for Kitty."

"And, of course, if she spent a week with you in London you would have an excuse for inviting a friend of hers to your dance too, wouldn't you?"

"Father is to be in Athens until the autumn of next

year," Meg went on thoughtfully. "And Mother will be with him this Christmas. Aunt Lizzie is coming to look after Bob and me. I adore Aunt Lizzie!"

"Because you know you can twist her round your little finger. A more easily swayed little body I've yet to find. It's a good thing Bob will be there because Heaven knows what you might be up to if you were alone with Aunt Liz."

They reached the entrance to The Gables and she paused by the gate to smooth the lapel of his coat. "I'll send you an invitation to my party if you promise not to be so cross!" she wheedled him.

"No, thank you." Deliberately he took her hands and put them down by her sides and moved on up the drive. "I'm not being a cat's paw again. What you do in London will be your own affair."

But it was not possible to maintain his annoyance in the face of her laughter, and during the next few days he discovered quite a liking for little Kitty Ralston and her friend Sidney Burke. They found a rickety tent in the stable loft at The Gables and erected it on the beach, so that they could use it in turn to change into their bathing suits, and for once the weather was kind and the wild seas of the bay became like a mill-pond under the August sun.

In the afternoons they fished for mackerel, or hired a sailing boat and took it across the bay to watch the Channel steamers come in, and after dinner Kitty and Sidney were invited to The Gables. And while Kitty played cribbage with old Lady Winter, Sidney was drawn over to the piano, where he played for Meg and her cousin to sing rollicking choruses from the Gilbert and Sullivan light operas until the dowager begged them to desist.

"How can Kitty and I concentrate on our game if you deafen us with all that noise?" she asked. "Mr. Burke, will you kindly accompany Meg in a quieter song. Something pleasantly sentimental, please."

Among the music in the rack they came upon a book of Scottish ballads, and gentleness fell on Sidney's hands as he played "Annie Laurie," while Meg's pretty voice rose over his playing like a lark.

"Charming," said the dowager, forgetting her cards. "Quite charming...You play very well, Mr. Burke."

"It was your grand-daughter's voice, Lady Winter," he said. "Nothing could spoil that." He got up, his eyes on Meg, but she made him sit down again.

"It is your turn to sing now," she protested. "You are not going to escape! What shall it be? 'Alice, where art thou?' or 'Auld Robin Grey'?"

"Neither." He pushed away the music, ran his fingers lightly over the keys, and then with his eyes on her lovely face in the light of the candles, he sang "There is a Lady sweet and kind," his light tenor voice caressingly soft, and yet the words so clear that the dowager stopped her game to listen, her old face soft too with tenderness.

> "There is a Lady sweet and kind
> Was never face so pleased my mind;
> I did but see her passing by
> And yet I love her till I die.
> Her gesture, motion, and her smiles
> Her wit, her voice my heart beguiles,
> Beguiles my heart, I know not why,
> And yet I love her till I die."

The voice stopped, the last note died away, and in the breathless little silence that followed Lady Winter said it was getting late, she was tired, and it was time Mr. Burke took Kitty home.

After they had gone and Meg had gone up to bed, the old lady told Richard he might enjoy a pipe or a cigar in the smoking room if he pleased before he retired. "They will have left brandy and soda there," she added, going with him to make sure that the decanter and the glasses were there on the silver tray. "Meg is going to be a sad flirt," she said before she left him. "You must marry her quickly, Richard, and take her to India with you."

"An army lieutenant does not marry unless he is a fool," he said smiling. "It will be seven years before I get my Captaincy, Aunt Margaret."

"Seven years!" His great-aunt sighed. "Too long for Meg to wait! But in the army I suppose there is a chance of sudden promotion in the event of war?"

"Are you thinking of this threatened war with Germany?"

"No, I don't believe that rubbish. If it were the French now, I might take it more seriously, in spite of the *entente cordiale*. But the Germans...no! I like them, always have, and when people tell me that we shall fight them I say, 'Don't you believe it. It's only that cocky Kaiser of theirs rattling his sabre. Edward the Peacemaker will put him in his place.'"

"I hope you are right."

"What about that Lestrange uncle of yours?" she went on, her thoughts returning to Meg. "The one that is to leave you all his money? Would he not do something for you now?"

"Not he!" Richard laughed. "He paid for my education and he gives me two hundred pounds a year because he knows that an army officer cannot live on his pay, but beyond that his attitude is 'Wait until I've gone.' And I don't blame him for it. But as he is a hale and hearty sixty, unless he breaks his neck out hunting I can see myself waiting a long time."

She was disappointed and changed the subject. "A pleasant young man, Mr. Burke, with a fine voice. Who is he?"

"A medical student." Richard rightly construed her question as meaning what was Mr. Burke. "His father is a music hall comedian and an old friend of Mrs. Ralston's."

"*That* vulgar little woman!" The dowager sniffed. "It's a pity young Burke doesn't go on the 'halls,' too: he would make more money than in medicine. I hope Meg won't wreck his career."

"Do you think she might?"

"Well, he is a nice lad, and in love with her. I've

seldom heard a more moving tribute to a girl of seventeen than that song he sang to her tonight.... Oh, yes, he sang it to her alone." She saw him smile. "You think I'm growing old and imagining things, and perhaps you are right.... Don't sit up too long." She kissed him goodnight and went away to her bed.

Richard sat over his brandy and soda thinking about his great-aunt's words: Meg accepted Sidney's devotion in her usual, light-hearted fashion, and he also felt sorry for the young man. Whichever way you looked at it, he was bound to get hurt.

On Sidney's last afternoon at Flint House a picnic had been planned in the woods on the Lewes Road. Effie promised to preside and told Clara to make some cakes.

"There's Sunday's plum cake not finished yet," said the old woman sourly. "I've only got one pair of 'ands."

That afternoon Effie dressed herself in her prettiest dress, of pink cotton, full of flounces and bows of ribbon and trails of lace, and if it was unsuitable for a picnic, at least the effect she made was striking as she stepped from the hired cab at the entrance to the woods where Meg and her cousin were waiting. Richard was curious to meet Kitty's mother, his interest having been aroused by Sidney's reluctance to discuss her, and by the dowager's dislike.

The new dress gave her confidence as she fell in beside him, and while Meg and Sidney and the young Ralstons went on ahead, the boys carrying the hamper between them, she began to recommend her daughter to his notice. Did he not think that Kitty was sweetly pretty, she asked? Of course she was only a schoolgirl as yet, but she was quite sure that in a few years' time she would be a raving beauty. She was so like what she was at that age, though with different colouring, of course. And she could tell him, in confidence, that she wouldn't be penniless either. She would come into quite a nice little income of her own one day. If she had pinned a ticket marked "Bargain For Young Men" in her daughter's hat, he thought with dismayed amusement, she could not have been more outspoken.

"When they reached the clearing where they planned to have their picnic she left him, much to his relief, and seated herself deliberately between Meg and Sidney, cutting across their light-hearted chatter and sending the young man to help Johnnie to fill the kettle from the stream.

"We don't want tadpoles in our tea," she said. "And you have monopolised Meg long enough. I want to talk to her now. Kitty dear, you can spread the cloth here on the grass and help Mr. Lestrange unpack the hamper." She smiled at Meg from under her large hat. "An old friend of mine has just moved out to Kensington, which isn't far from where you live, is it?"

"Not very far," said Meg.

"Your mother probably knows her already," said Effie. "Her husband is the famous artist, Sir William Faulkner. Everybody is running after him these days. Lady F. is a great friend of mine, and her children often played in the garden with Kit and Johnnie when we lived in Willowbrook Road, didn't they, Kit?"

Kitty smiled but did not answer: the spreading of the lace-trimmed cloth over the rough grass was causing her a little trouble. Meg said that she did not think her mother knew Lady Faulkner.

"Not know her? I am surprised!" Effie gave a small, affected laugh. "I thought everybody in London knew Sir William and Lady Faulkner. They have scores of friends. I know when I go and stay with them while the children are at school we never dine at home. We are always being asked out somewhere, night after night."

Kitty raising her head from her cloth-spreading, saw Meg's eyes meet Richard's for a fleeting second in half-laughing concern, and Effie saw the glance too and took offence.

"Perhaps Belgravia does not include Kensington in its visiting list?" she said with a sneer.

"Not at all." Meg hesitated and then added with a little air of dignity that annoyed Effie still more, "But

I think Sir William was divorced by his first wife so that he could marry the present Lady Faulkner, and my mother doesn't call on divorced people."

Fortunately Richard chose that moment to win his battle with the hamper straps and called on Kitty for instructions as to where plates and cups were to be placed. Johnnie and Sidney came back with the filled kettle, and a great deal of laughter and excitement was caused by the lighting of a fire beneath it, and Kitty put out the thick sandwiches, heavy scones and the large plum cake over from Sunday, that had been Clara's idea of what they should eat at a picnic.

As she watched her daughter Effie was savagely glad that the fare was not more elegant. Why should they put themselves out for these stuck-up Winters? Not call on divorced people indeed, when everyone knew what the first Lady F. was like and the hell she gave her husband for years!

Seeing that she was offended Richard hastily introduced a new topic of conversation. "Did Meg tell you," he asked, "that she is thinking of becoming a Suffragette?"

"Richard that is not true!" cried Meg. "Don't listen to him, Mrs. Ralston! I went to a political meeting with Daisy and her eldest sister Flora during the Easter holidays and Rick went with us. Violet refused to come."

"And I wouldn't have come either, had I known what Flora intended to do," said Richard.

"Why?" Sidney was watching the gold of the dappled sunlight touching the hair under Meg's straw hat. "What happened?"

"I ought to have known something was in the wind when Meg was so anxious to go," grumbled Richard. "Anyway, just as Mr. Balfour got up to speak this woman, Flora Drayton, jumped up and screamed out, 'What about the vote for women? When are you going to give us that?'"

Meg's eyes met Sidney's mirthfully. "We were thrown

out," she said with a joyous laugh. "It was the greatest fun in the world."

"I don't see how you can say that when Daisy was terrified, poor child, and I had a split lip and a torn jacket in trying to protect you both. The stewards set about me as if I were Mrs. Pankhurst herself."

"He told Mother that the horse fell down in the cab coming home," said Meg with another gurgle of laughter. "If ever I join the Suffragettes I shall not ask you to come to my meetings, Rick. I shall get Sidney to escort me."

Sidney here said hastily that politics were not in his line.

"What cowards men are!" sighed Meg.

"Of course Flora Drayton is so plain and such a frump that the only way she can draw attention to herself is by creating disturbances at meetings," Richard said cruelly. "Nobody in his right mind would want to marry her."

"Most career women are plain," said Sidney sweepingly. "You should see some of the females who are qualifying as doctors these days. Mind you, they are clever. But then it doesn't matter about a beautiful woman being stupid. She will always find a husband."

"I agree with you, Sidney," Effie said, tipping the tea into the tea-pot. "Women should be beautiful and leave politics alone. I'm sure you wouldn't like your wife to have a vote, would you, Mr. Lestrange?"

"I should hate it," said Richard promptly. "Unless she voted as I told her, of course."

"And then you'd have two votes instead of one," cried Meg. "Which would be grossly unfair."

"Not at all. She would simply acknowledge my superior intellect. But I can see our kettle boiling, and I will fetch it for our tea." As he came back with it Effie smiled her thanks at him from under her shady hat and he thought how pretty she was, although the light, frilly dress would have been more suitable on her daughter. "I was asking Kitty the other day if she was related to my brother-in-law," he said pleasantly, as

93

Effie held out the tea-pot for the water. "Did your husband ever speak to you of Stephen Ralston Brett?" And then he broke off with an exclamation of alarm, as the tea-pot gave a lurch, and the boiling water missed it and nearly caught her hand instead. "My dear Mrs. Ralston, don't say I have scalded you hand with my clumsiness?"

"No, it went on the cloth. No harm is done." She put the tea-pot down. "It was my fault. I should have put it on the ground in the first place. It is quite safe now, Mr. Lestrange."

"You are sure your hand wasn't touched?" he asked anxiously.

"No, indeed it wasn't. See for yourself!" She held out a pretty hand, over-loaded with jewellery, for his inspection, laughing over his concern.

"It is always a mistake to talk to a lady when she is making tea," said Sidney loudly. "It is the serious event of the day. You should know that by now."

Effie began to pour the tea into the cups. "You were saying something about your brother-in-law, I believe, Mr. Lestrange?" she said lightly. "I didn't catch his name..."

Richard repeated it. Effie told Johnnie to hand round the milk and sugar. "No," she said, "I don't think my husband ever mentioned that name to me, but I daresay there are a lot of Ralstons in the world, you know. I have noticed that before. You meet somebody with an extraordinary name, and you think there could not be two people with it, and then a housemaid will apply for a situation, or the butcher has an aunt, or the laundry woman a sister, with the same name."

She chatted on, and as she sipped her tea and said it tasted of wood-smoke, and asked Sidney to cut the cake, from the place he had been given beside Kitty Richard watched her and thought that she was a cool piece.

"I'll swear she has heard of Stephen," he told himself.

"And I wonder what it was that her husband did—beside marrying her—that put him outside the pale?" He would so very much like to discover a black sheep in his brother-in-law's family.

10

Meg carried out her intention of inviting Kitty to spend a week of the Christmas holidays with her.

"I don't see why Kitty should not stay with you, dear," her easy-going aunt said. "It would be nice if you could arrange her visit to coincide with your little dance on New Year's Eve."

"That is what I thought I would do," said Meg.

Kitty never forgot that week, even if the night of the dance came within an ace of spoiling it. Every moment was a sheer delight, with visits to the theatre, to picture galleries, to concerts and to parties at the houses of the Winters' friends. And to round it off there was the dance on New Year's Eve attended by about a hundred young people.

"I always seem to be apologising for being late when I'm invited to a dance," Sidney told Meg when he made an unexpected appearance half-way through the evening. "But there is a pea-souper in Hampstead tonight and no cabs will stir out."

"As long as you are here," smiled Meg. "That is all that matters."

Kitty assumed that the list of their guests had been compiled by Bob and his sister together, and she was astonished when he undeceived her a couple of dances later.

"I know this is our dance, Kitty," he said, rather stiff and unsmiling as he stood before her. "But do you mind if we don't dance just yet?"

He took her into the deserted library and closed the door. "I think you must have forgotten a conversation we once had about your friend Mr. Burke being invited here?" he said, his voice quiet and his nice face more grieved than angry.

She stared at him in bewilderment. "I'm afraid I don't understand you," she said.

"Oh, Kitty, my dear little girl!" He walked to the fire and stood there with his back to it, his slender frame very erect. "When he arrived just now I asked Meg what in Heaven's name he was doing here, and she said she was very sorry, she knew I'd be angry, but that you had asked her to invite him and she had not liked to refuse."

"Meg said...*what*?" Kitty sat down on the arm of one of the leather arm-chairs, feeling as if her legs would give way beneath her.

"Surely there must have been several of your school-friends you could have invited instead of young Burke?" he went on. "You knew how much I would dislike having him here."

"But..." Kitty felt her indignation rising. "Quite apart from who asked him, Bob, if he was good enough for your grandmother to invite to her house, why shouldn't he be good enough for you?"

"I beg your pardon?" His astonishment showed in his face. "Kitty, are you seriously telling me that Burke went to The Gables? When did this happen pray?"

"Last August, when you were in Switzerland and Sidney was staying with us at Flint House."

"Of course, Meg and Richard were staying with

Grandmamma at that time." His stiff manner dropped from him like a shed garment. "Kitty, did Meg know that Sidney Burke was to be with you in White Cliff Bay?"

"I don't know, but I daresay he may have told her at the end of term ball. He was my partner for that night. Perhaps she did not tell you that? Anyway we used to meet on the beach and go swimming together and that sort of thing, and Lady Winter invited Sidney and me to her house nearly every evening while Meg and Richard were there. I played cribbage with your grandmother, while the others sang round the piano and Lady Winter seemed to enjoy it as much as we did. When she said goodbye to Sidney she said she hoped she would seem him again."

"The devil she did!" Bob was disconcerted. "I wasn't told about your end of term ball, nor about Burke being in White Cliff Bay later, and as I have been up at Oxford since October and Richard has not been here this Christmas, unless Meg had told me there was no way in which I could find out."

"I had no idea that Sidney was coming here tonight," Kitty said honestly. "I would never be so impertinent as to ask my friends to your dance. Surely you know that, Bob?"

"But of course I do," he said, and suddenly he smiled and the warmth in his face lifted the dismay from her heart. "And I beg your pardon, Kitty, for having thought otherwise. I ought to have known you—and Meg—better than that. I hope you will show your forgiveness by coming and finishing our dance?"

She went back happily with him to the dance-room, but although outwardly she was as light-hearted as before, inwardly Meg's behavior teased and hurt her. It was not the first time that her friend had shown her the deceitful side of her character, a side that she hated while she continued to love her. She had the next dance with Sidney, but her thoughts were elsewhere and presently he glanced down at her with half-humourous concern.

"What has happened?" he asked. "When I first saw you this evening you were sparkling in your pretty party dress like a Christmas fairy. But now you are quiet, and you've lost your sparkle, and your eyes look...bruised. What is the matter, Sugar Mouse?"

His friendly voice made her catch her breath and tears almost forced themselves to her eyes, but she managed to repress them and to assure him that there was nothing the matter, that she was enjoying herself enormously, and didn't he think the floor was lovely, and that she and Bob and Meg had spent the afternoon helping the footmen to polish it. And all the time she was talking she knew that he had forgotten her already, and that he was only watching Meg across the room.

That night, after the New Year had been toasted in champagne cup and the carriages waiting in the square had been summoned to take the guests home, Kitty followed Meg to her room.

"Why did you lie to Bob, Meg?" she asked quietly. "Surely it would have been simpler to tell him that you had invited Sidney here tonight? When he knew that he had been to your grandmother's house last August he agreed that there was no reason why he should not come."

Meg had the grace to look slightly ashamed.

"I'm sorry, darling," she said penitently. "It was horrid of me to drag you into it, but you see I hadn't told Bob that I saw Sidney in White Cliff Bay because I knew he'd think...Oh, well, what does it matter what he thinks? He's such a conventional sort of person, and he never liked poor Sidney. I had to invent some sort of excuse for having him here, hadn't I?" Her voice became more caressing. "Don't say you *mind*, darling? What are friends for if not to help each other?"

Kitty could not see how she had been helped by Meg that evening, and she was not cajoled into easy forgiveness. "Is that why you asked me here?" she said bluntly. "So that you could invite Sidney to your party tonight?"

"Of course not!" But Meg's indignation did not ring quite true. "Fancy even thinking such a thing, you great goose! I asked you because I wanted you to come, and I thought it was time you had some fun. And you have enjoyed it, haven't you, Kit? Do say you have, or I shall be utterly miserable."

Kitty was unable to hold out any longer. "Of course I've enjoyed it," she said.

"Then there's nothing more to worry about, is there?" Meg hugged her affectionately and rang the bell for her maid. "Shall I send Everett to you when I've finished?"

"No, thank you. I can unhook myself." Kitty went away to her room, but for a long time after she was in bed she lay in the dark wondering how a nature like Meg's could be at once so generous and so mean, and she hoped that Sidney was not as much in love with her as she feared he was, and she knew that there was nothing she could do to stop it if he was. And then finally, just before she dropped off to sleep, the warm memory of Bob came like balm to her spirit. He was as fine as his sister was fickle, as open as she was underhand: in Bob there was somebody who would always help if she needed it, who would stand like a rock in times of trouble, where Sidney would smile, pat her shoulder, and hurry away.

She went home the next day by a noon-day train, and Bob saw her off at Victoria and made sure that the footman supplied her with the small luncheon hamper that had been packed for her by the still-room maid. It was a delicious lunch of chicken sandwiches and hard-boiled eggs and mince pies, wrapped up neatly in spotless table napkins, with a small bottle or red wine to keep out the cold of the January day.

As Kitty ate and drank she wished she had not been so silent before the train had taken her away: she would have given anything in those last few minutes with Bob to be able to chatter like Meg.

When she arrived at White Cliff Bay Johnnie was at the station to meet her, and he suggested that they should send her luggage up by the luggage cart and walk.

"We've had the most awful gales down here since you have been away," he told her. "And the sea looks ripping today. The waves are mountains high, and you'll have to hold on to me if you don't want to be blown off your feet. There was a cab bowled clean over this morning on the front."

"Don't let's risk our lives in a cab then!" Kitty tucked her hand into his arm and thought what a nice person he was growing into. "What have you been doing with yourself while I've been away? Have you thought any more about what you are going to be?"

"Oh, I'd like to be a soldier, of course, like Father. But Mother says that if you are an officer you need a lot of private means. I don't think Mr. Lestrange is very rich though."

"He isn't, but he has a wealthy old uncle in the background." Kitty studied her brother thoughtfully. "Have you spoken to Mr. Grant about it?"

"Yes. He said that when I'm thirteen next summer I shan't be able to go on at St. David's any longer. He wanted to know what public school I was down for, but when I asked Mother she said she hadn't thought about it."

"But Johnnie, love, she must think about it. You've got to go to a public school!"

"Yes, I suppose so." He hesitated and then he burst out, "It's that chap Calverley Ricketts being here so often. She can't think of anything else."

"Mr. Ricketts? Down here? Are you sure, Johnnie?"

"Of course I'm sure. You needn't look so astonished, Kit. He's here again today, which is partly why I came to meet you. I knew Mother wouldn't like you to arrive suddenly while he was here."

"But Johnnie..." Kitty was frowning now. "How often does he come?"

"He came nearly every Sunday last term. I think he's trying to persuade Mother to go back to the stage: he keeps giving her presents."

"What sort of presents?"

"Oh, gold bracelets and a diamond watch...things like that."

"Oh, no!" Kitty was horrified. "She couldn't take expensive jewellery from...from..."

"Well, she does take it," said Johnnie bluntly. "And I don't see why she shouldn't, if he wants to give it to her. But I wish he didn't hate me so much!"

"Hate *you*? My dear old boy, why on earth should Mr. Ricketts hate you?"

"I don't know why he should, but he does! If I happen to meet him in the hall he looks through me as if I'm not there, and if I speak to him he doesn't answer."

"How mannerless of him!" Kitty was indignant.

"No. He just hates me. I know he does, because when he started coming Mother asked me if I'd mind having my dinner with Clara in the kitchen while Mr. Ricketts was here. I didn't mind...at least not much. I like old Clara. But there wasn't much sense in coming out for the day from school if I wasn't to see Mother, so I asked Mr. Grant if I could stay at school over Sundays, because Mother usually had a friend to see her then. He was awfully nice about it. He put his hand on my shoulder in a kind sort of way and said he would be pleased to have me. I think he knew about Mr. Ricketts already somehow, only I don't see how he could."

Kitty listened to Johnnie's outburst with growing indignation, not unmixed with alarm. If Mr. Grant knew about Calverley Ricketts' visits to their mother, then most certainly his sister knew, and with her the whole of the town.

Small things to which she had not paid any attention at the time came back to her: in the few days when she was at home over Christmas before she went to London, she had noticed a marked coolness in the greetings of the few friends they had in the place, and the interest they had shown in shop windows as she approached had been distinctly unusual. And then there was the Webbers' invitation that had not come.

Every year, since they had settled in White Cliff

Bay, there had been one festivity upon which they could count, and that was the Christmas party at the lawyer's house in Broad Street. Kindly Mrs. Webber had no children of her own, and she invited all the young people of the town to her party, and until this year Kitty and her brother had been included. But this Christmas when no invitation arrived they had thought that Mrs. Webber was abandoning her parties: now Kitty knew that all that had happened was that she had crossed the young Ralstons off her list.

With anger burning in her heart she turned up Fish Lane with Johnnie and came out upon the sea-front.

"I suppose we'd better go in by the back way in case he's still there?" said Johnnie.

"Certainly not!" Kitty caught his hand firmly in hers. "We will go in the front way, and if we meet Mr. Ricketts in the hall we will teach him his manners!"

But when they opened the front door Johnnie was relieved to see that the silk hat, and the fur-collared overcoat, the lavender gloves and the gold-headed malacca cane that he had come to associate with Calverley Ricketts were gone and their owner with them.

From the little he had seen of him he guessed that the great actor was not a patient man, and in her present mood there was no knowing what Kitty might have said or done.

11

During their last term at Miss Westlake's, as senior girls of the school, Kitty and Meg were allowed a great deal more freedom.

Cabs were hired to take them to special music and singing lessons, to art classes, and for visits to galleries and museums, with the French teacher, Mlle. Gaudet, to chaperone them.

To Kitty's secret relief they now had separate rooms, and although Meg's room was superior to hers, which had never been more than a box-room, she liked to have her own things about her, although she missed her friend's chatter as an accompaniment to her dressing.

Ever since New Year's Eve she had felt that she could not trust Meg, and before long she realised that Meg had asked for her own room, and that when she sat at her little writing-table in the evenings, it was not the day's study that kept her busy, but the writing of numerous notes to young men: notes that she bribed one of the housemaids to post for her.

One afternoon they had gone to the National Gallery

to see the new Valasquez, "Venus and Cupid," the girls very grown up with their long skirts, and Meg looking very charming in a little new fur hat. As Mlle. Gaudet stopped behind to pay the cabby a young man ran down the steps with a smile of welcome.

"Why Sidney!" cried Kitty. "I did not expect to see you here. Since when have you been interested in art?" And then she glanced at Meg and the reason for the little fur hat suddenly became clear.

"There are some sides to Sidney that are most unexpected, Kitty dear!" said Meg with a laugh, and taking his arm she walked off, leaving her to follow with Mademoiselle.

"This Mr. Burke, he is a relative of Miss Winter's family?" asked the governess uneasily, conscious of her responsibility for her pupils' behaviour.

"No," said Kitty with a touch of restraint. "He is an old friend of mine."

"Of *yours*?" The little Frenchwoman was astonished. "But why then does he not give his arm to you, ma cherie?" She glanced from Kitty to the two in front of them with a droll expression. "If a young man as handsome as this Mr. Burke were my friend, I would not give him up so lightly, Miss Ralston!" After a moment, however, she added more thoughtfully, "But Miss Winter is a very wealthy young lady, is she not? And her father is a very important gentleman. It makes a difference to a young man, that!"

In the old days Kitty would have replied that things like that did not count with Sidney, but now she felt that she did not know him any more. The old Sidney would not have dreamt of making secret assignations with a girl like Meg.

That night, during study hour, she went to Meg's room and asked if she could speak to her.

"Of course. Come in, darling. I don't know why this is called a 'study' hour, because I never study anything in it!" Meg's laughing face was as innocent as a lamb, and Kitty came into the room and shut the door.

"Meg," she said, "did you arrange to meet Sidney today?"

"Of course I didn't." Meg saw relief struggling with disbelief in her friend's open countenance and burst out laughing. "Oh, well, perhaps I did mention that we might be at the National Gallery this afternoon. But how was I to know that he would be there, too?" Kitty remained silent and she glanced at her impatiently. "Why are you so dreadfully serious over everything, Kit? I mean to have some fun for my last few weeks here, and if Mr. Burke likes to share that fun I am not going to stop him. I couldn't if I tried! He is desperately in love with me."

"But are you in love with him?"

"Don't be absurd, darling! As if I would fall in love with a medical student!"

"Then you should leave him alone!" Kitty was indignant with her for her heartlessness. "Meg, don't you see what you are doing? You are taking him away from his work when he can't afford to fail his exams. He is not the son of a rich man, he's the son of an actor, and as long as actors are in work everything is fine, but when they are 'resting' they starve. In kindness to Sid and his parents, Meg dear, please leave him alone!"

Meg, who had been sitting looking out of the window, now got up and drew the curtains to shut out the street lamps, and turned to her with a slightly mocking smile. "Poor Kitty!" she said. "Do I detect a touch of the green-eyed monster in your concern for Mr. Burke?"

Kitty did not reply and Meg went on in the same light way: "It is very hard that he should prefer me to you, but that isn't my fault, darling. You should try to be more lively when you are with young men. To get a reputation for being dull is the one unforgivable crime."

"I think I'd rather be dull than cruel," Kitty said gently, and went away to her room.

Meg did not hold her protest against her, and at breakfast next morning she showed her a letter she had had from her mother, in which Lady Winter said she hoped to be home in April. "And directly she is home everything will be put in hand for my coming out dance in June," Meg added, her eyes sparkling. "It will be in the same week that I am to be presented, and I shall die of excitement. My curtsey is nearly perfect."

The senior girls had been practising their Court curtseys during their dancing lessons, ready for the Season ahead, and Kitty had practised with them although hers would not be needed.

"It's a pity you are not going to be presented, Kit," Meg said. "But unless you marry somebody important I don't suppose you ever will be."

"And I'm not likely to do that," said Kitty crisply.

"You never know. You might meet someone who would fall in love with you and marry you in a week," said Meg more seriously. "An aunt of mine eloped with a postman."

"Are you suggesting that I should do the same? Because the postman who delivers our letters here is at least a hundred years old, and the one in White Cliff Bay is the father of twelve. I cannot imagine eloping with either of those gentlemen."

Meg laughed again joyously. "Well, anyway you will come to my coming-out ball," she said. "And Mother will bring a string of eligible young men to write their names on your programme."

For a few days the girls were back on their old happy terms, and then once more Meg began using Kitty as a screen for her activities. One afternoon when they set out to attend an art class at a studio in St. John's Wood, she sent a note by Kitty to say that she was prevented from being there that day, and she took the cab on to a destination known only to herself. As the artist who taught them was a lady it had not been thought necessary for the hard-worked Mlle Gaudet to act as chaperone, and Meg had known it and laid her plans accordingly.

"Don't you want to know where I've been?" she asked teasingly, when she picked Kitty up again an hour or so later.

"I expect you have been meeting a young man," said Kitty resignedly. "It is none of my business."

"Oh, don't be so unfeeling!" Meg thrust her hand into her arm and gave it an impatient little squeeze. "It was only a bit of fun, but if you are going to be stupid about it I shall not tell you anything. And anyway I think your Sidney is like you—far too serious over trifles."

"So it was Sidney you went to see?" said Kitty quickly.

"Yes, I went to his rooms, and you needn't look so horrified. His dreadful old landlady insisted on keeping the door of his sitting-room open all the time I was there, so that she could hear what we were talking about."

"I daresay she thought Sidney needed a chaperone," said Kitty drily. He had taken those rooms in order to work later and longer hours. "Have you asked him to your ball?"

"No, but I daresay I shall, although as the ballroom is to be opened up and a floor laid over the lawn at the back, and there will be hundreds of people there, I don't suppose I shall even *see* him—if he comes."

"If you ask him nothing would keep him away."

"Well, he can dance with you this time. When people start taking me for granted they have to be taught a lesson."

"If Sidney has been taking you for granted I expect you have given him every reason for doing so."

"Perhaps I have," agreed Meg calmly. "But I don't know how he could think that I would get *engaged* to him, before I've had any fun at all! I know a lot of girls get engaged in their first season, but I don't intend to— I mean to enjoy myself first."

Kitty's heart sank. "So Sidney asked you to marry him?" she said.

"Why yes. He was all fiery devotion and that sort of thing. He knew he wasn't worthy of me, but he'd love me for ever, and so on... Mind you, I didn't refuse him right away." Meg's laughter was as brittle as glass. "I became feminine and fluttery, I said I must have

108

time to think about it, and that I didn't think I was old enough to marry anybody just yet." The cab stopped outside the school: it was nearly six o'clock and dusk was creeping into the streets, but in the light of the lamps she saw Kitty's face. "Don't look so woe-begone, darling! You can have him back again now!"

"Thank you, but I don't think I want him." The Sidney Burke that Kitty had known from childhood could not be handed back, like an unwanted cake on a plate, and as she climbed the stairs to her little room at the top she remembered the first day he had met Meg in White Cliff Bay and how Bob had warned her about his sister's habit of stealing from her friends, and for the first time since she had known her she felt she would be glad to have done with Meg and her pretty, heartless ways.

It was Effie who insisted on Kitty's acceptance of the invitation to Meg's coming-out ball.

"Of course you must go," she said. "I can't think why you hesitate. You say you haven't quarrelled with Meg? Well then you must go. It would be stupid to lose sight of the Winters now. We'll pop over to Brighton one day this week and order your dress. It will have to be in white I suppose, although I have a very pretty pink one that would fit you with very little alteration."

The dress came home from the dressmaker's, and although the cut and style reminded Kitty a little of the stage, the trailing white chiffon flounces with their knots of pink and white daisies were very pretty, and she put it on and stood on a sheet in the drawing-room while Effie studied her critically.

"Don't forget to catch up the train when you are dancing," she warned her. "I think you must wear your hair in the Pompadour style. It is young and becoming and will be easy for you to do. Those white suede gloves I've lent you should be pulled up above your elbows. Girls' elbows are never very pretty. You will need some jewellery. You can borrow some of mine."

Kitty said that she was going to wear the locket that Meg had given her for a parting present.

"Oh, that poor little thing!" said Effie contemptuously. "You can wear it if you like. I suppose you are too young for diamonds!" She said no more, but on the following day as she helped her to pack she said unexpectedly: "If I were in your shoes I'd make a dead set at young Lestrange."

"At Richard?" Kitty laughed. "Mother, he's head over ears in love with Meg and always has been."

"Then you want to cut her out with him, my girl, as she cut you out with Sid, nasty little cat." As Kitty did not answer Effie went on, "What would make me really laugh would be if you were to marry Bob."

Kitty bent her head over a sheet of tissue paper, smoothing it over the train of the ball-dress before she folded it. "What is there so funny about that?" she asked.

"Oh, it would score off somebody I know, that's all." Effie said airly. "No matter who...or why."

Kitty went off to London with mixed feelings, in which uneasiness and apprehension almost outweighed any pleasurable anticipation of the evening, but when she arrived in Belgrave Square that afternoon and saw among the young people there one well-remembered face all apprehension left her.

"Little Kitty with her hair up!" Bob said smiling. "I shall miss your long plait all the same."

"Wait till I take my hat off!" she warned him. "It will descend then in a shower of pins."

"It is very becoming," he said gravely. "I wonder what Burke will think of it?"

"Sidney?" She looked up quickly. "He is coming then?"

"Yes. Meg asked Mother to invite him." He hesitated. "She means to give him his congé tonight, poor chap." As she was silent he went on gently, "Believe me, Kitty, it is kinder in the end. The fellow has been hanging round her long enough, and she has only been amusing herself."

"I know." But Kitty's eyes were troubled. "I wish though for Sidney's sake that it hadn't got to end like this."

"Do you really wish that?" He looked surprised, and seemed about to say something more and then changed his mind. "I should say he will find it easy to console himself, all the same."

"But you don't know him, Bob. I don't think he'll forget Meg quickly."

"Then he's a greater fool than I take him for," he said, and as Richard Lestrange came up to them he moved away.

Kitty was glad to find that Richard was her partner at dinner that night: his pleasant, cheerful manner dispelled the shyness that attacked her among so many strangers.

"How is that young brother of yours?" he asked as they sat down. "Is he still keen on going into the army?"

"Oh, yes, but I'm afraid Mother will not be able to afford it as a career for Johnnie."

"Then he must join the Volunteers. They go out on manoeuvers and practice drill and rifle-shooting for hours on end at their local drill halls. He'd enjoy it no end, and if there was a war he'd probably be commissioned right away."

"A war?" Her mind went to South Africa.

"That's what soldiers are paid for," he reminded her whimsically. "To fight for King and Country!"

"I daresay, but I hope Johnnie will find something more peaceful to occupy his time. We don't even know what public school he is going to yet."

"Indeed?" Richard was politely shocked. "Wasn't he put down for one when he was born?"

"No." She hesitated and added, "My father was at Eton. Mother let it slip out one day when I was talking about schools, but why Johnnie was not put down for it too I don't know." She paused and then went on smiling, "But here is the fish, which means that I must turn my attention to my other neighbour. He looks a dreadfully important old gentleman. Do you know who he is?"

He glanced past her, "Sir Algernon Symes, an old friend of Bob's father. He is taking Bob to Paris in the autumn to teach him the ropes."

"Is Bob going into the Diplomatic Service too then, now that he has left Oxford?"

"He is, dear old fellow." Richard glanced across the table at his cousin with a mixture of affection and respect. "He's one of the bravest people I know." And then the young woman on his other side claimed his attention and she was left to entertain Sir Algernon.

She did not find it as difficult as she had anticipated, because in hunting about for a suitable subject of conversation she hit upon the Channel Tunnel. Did he think, she asked, that it would really come to nothing?

He turned to regard his young neighbour with a light of interest in his twinkling eyes. Yes, he said, he was very sure it would, and he was ready to promise that when it came up in the House for serious discussion next year it would be dismissed for good and all. And an excellent thing too, he added, warming to his subject: apart from the military and naval dangers and the extra spending it would incur in those services, he could see no prospect of any advantage being gained by the trade of the country. And that, after all, was the main reason for the project in the first place.

Kitty, delighted at having hit on a topic of such interest to her old neighbour, ate fish and threw in a word of wonder, admiration and assent from time to time, and was almost set off laughing when her eyes caught Bob's unexpectedly.

"Who taught you to entertain old gentlemen so well?" he asked her later as he scribbled his initials against several dances on her programme. "Sir Algy is full of your praises. 'Who is the charmin' little lady I was talking to at dinner?' he said. I had great pleasure in telling him."

"But it was easy!" Her cheeks were flushed and her

eyes shining. "I simply let him talk about a thing that interested him."

"It worked well with Sir Algy," he agreed. "But if you had been next to a gourmet you might have had to do the talking."

"Then I'd have told him about the mackerel we catch in White Cliff Bay, and the way Clara fries them, split open and crisp and golden. It is the one thing she can cook well." She was suddenly confused at the look in his smiling eyes. "Is my hair coming down?"

"It is beautifully neat." He handed her programme back to her. "I was thinking how charming that dress is with its little knots of daisies. You look a little like Cinderella waiting for the clock to strike twelve."

"Perhaps I am," she said suddenly serious. "Waiting for the clock to strike twelve."

"That was sadly said," he remarked gently. "I hope it doesn't mean that when tonight is over Meg will lose her best friend? She—we—would miss you a great deal, Kitty, if that should happen." And then his Aunt Liz, who had taken Kitty under her wing for the evening, brought up a number of young men to be introduced, and Bob went to ask Violet Drayton for a dance.

Kitty felt her spirits lift as she went on to the floor with Richard a little later: the banks of flowers, the dresses and the jewels, the Hungarian band with its lovely music, were intoxicating, her partner was one of the nicest young men she knew after Bob, and this was the first grown-up occasion of her life. She gave herself up to enjoyment, and when the waltz finished she accompanied her partner to Lady Winter's drawing-room to sit down before the next dance, and complimented him on the improvement in his dancing.

"You did not tread on my toes once," she said.

"You are kinder than Meg then. The best she could find to say in my praise was that I did not tread on her toes quite so often!" He went on after a moment, "I have been admiring your locket. I don't think I've seen such a pretty one before."

The trinket of which Effie had been so contemptuous

had a design of forget-me-nots in turquoise and pearls set in gold, and it was suspended round Kitty's neck on a slender gold chain. She told him that Meg had given it to her.

"I felt so shabby at having such a beautiful present from her," she added. "When I only gave her a book of Tennyson's poems."

"'Come into the garden, Maud,'" quoted Richard. "Or did Wordsworth write that? Don't know much about poets—not gentry I care for much, I'm afraid. They don't cut their hair."

She laughed with him. Dear Richard, to talk nonsense, and dear Meg, to give her this lovely locket. "Isn't it pretty?" she said, lifting it in her fingers. "And you can't see what is in it either, which is a good thing."

"Don't tell me you've got a sweetheart's face tucked away in it?" he teased her.

"No, I have not then." She slipped the chain off her neck and showed it to him in the palm of her hand. "You see, ever since my father was killed my mother would not have a photograph of him in the house—I believe a sudden loss will affect people like that. But I had one, unknown to my mother, and Meg knew it, and that is why she gave me this locket. It exactly fits the face in my photograph, so that now I've left school I need not keep my beloved father hidden away any longer. I can wear him round my neck as my greatest treasure." She pressed the little spring that released the pretty, ornamented front. "You can see him if you like."

He took the opened locket and studied the pictured face inside, and as he did so Kitty saw his own face go curiously still, and his smile faded, and she knew in that moment that he had recognized it.

"You have seen it before?" she cried breathlessly.

He nodded. "Oh, yes," he said quietly. "I've seen that face before." He closed the locket with a snap and handed it back to her.

"And you've seen it at Cranston?" she pursued, delighted. "Oh, Richard!...My father *was* related to your brother-in-law!"

It was a moment or two before he replied and then he said carefully: "I should say that my brother-in-law knew him as well as most people—if not better. But I'm afraid I can't tell you any more than that." And he took her back to the ballroom.

12

Kitty had to sit for some minutes among the wallflowers before Sidney came to claim her for their dance.

"I'd almost given you up," she said, her feet impatient to begin.

"I couldn't find you in all this crush." He regarded the crowded floor with disgust. "Can't we sit it out?"

"If you prefer it." She was disappointed.

"I do indeed." It had been arranged that Kitty was to leave Belgrave Square on the following day and go to Maidie for a night or two before going home, and as Sidney accompanied her back to the drawing-room, now almost empty, he told her that his mother was looking forward to seeing her.

"I've just been dancing with your little friend, Daisy Drayton," he went on as they found two chairs in a corner under a palm. "Do you know that sister of hers has persuaded her to march to Challoner Square tomorrow, as part of Mrs. Pankhurst's new militant campaign?"

"Challoner Square? What on earth for?"

"It's where the Lord Chancellor lives, and I don't know what they hope to gain by attacking *him*. I have seen some of the results of such attacks in hospital though, and they are anything but edifying."

"Oh, dear!" she looked at him apprehensively. "What do you think will happen tomorrow then?"

"I know what will happen. These Suffragists—or Suffragettes as the *Daily Mail* persists in calling them—go into action like trained troops, not counting the cost. They glory in it."

"Glory in what, Sid?"

"Why, in bruises and cuts, hair torn out, clothes ripped to pieces, arrest and prison for creating disturbances and obstructing the law."

"Oh, my goodness!" Kitty was dismayed. "And poor little Daisy will face that tomorrow? She can't know what is ahead of her."

"Violet has done her best to stop her, but I gather that she is quite determined."

"Daisy was never determined over anything in her life!" Kitty had long ago forgotten her first dislike for Daisy, who had grown up into a pretty little creature with an indeterminate air and a helpless way with her that was curiously attractive, but she was under no illusions about her. "Anybody could sway her into doing what they wanted her to do, and I thought this might happen when she left school and got into Flora's clutches. She will be swept away and trampled under her sister's sensible boots. Flora always wears *such* sensible boots!"

"More effective to kick policemen, my dear!"

"Oh, don't!" Kitty was distressed for Daisy. "This is awful. Do you think I could call in at Challoner Square on my way to Hampstead tomorrow and try to find her?"

"I wouldn't. You'll be put in prison too as an aider and abettor."

"Well, will you come with me then?"

"What, and cut a lecture? No thank you, my dear!"

She thought that if it had been Meg who had asked

him he would not have given the lecture a second's consideration. She asked gently, "Sid, has Meg danced with you tonight?"

"She has. We waltzed together most sedately, and as we danced she told me in the most charming way that she had no further use for my services. But then Meg is a very charming person. She dismissed me as if I were *quite* her favourite footman."

"Oh, Sid, I'm sorry!" She put out her hand to him but he did not see it. He was staring in front of him, seeing only Meg.

"When you come to think of it," he went on after a moment "her attitude is scarcely surprising. When I qualify in a few years' time all there is ahead of me is an assistant's post to some old country G.P. until I've saved enough to buy a practice or set up on my own. How could I expect a girl like Meg to take me seriously?... Tonight she has the world at her feet: everybody is saying how lovely she is and the men are round her like bees round a honey-pot." His hands were gently tearing his dance programme to strips as he spoke. "It was good of her to spare me one dance tonight—if only to say goodbye. In a week's time I shall borrow a silk hat and call upon Lady Winter, and having done the polite I shall cross Belgrave Square off my visiting list. It won't be too difficult." His voice was so bitter that it hurt. Kitty tried to find words to comfort him.

"If Meg meant nothing, why did she...why..."

"Why did she encourage me?" He smiled but there was no humour in his face. "I expect because she was bored and needed amusement. Young women like Meg always need amusement...And now we had better go back to the ballroom and when our dance is over I shall go."

"But Sid, we're not half-way through the evening yet!"

"My dear Sugar Mouse, they will not even know that I have gone!" He looked round him and put the pieces of his programme with its little tasselled pencil into a large bowl of white roses. "So pure!" he said, touching

118

the petals mockingly. "I hope the lead in the pencil won't kill them...but it's only a very little one after all."

As he edged out of the ballroom a little while later Kitty wished that he had said something about her dress. But all he would talk about was Daisy, and all he could think about was Meg...A friendly voice at her elbow recalled her to her surroundings. "Did I see young Burke deserting you, Kitty?"

"Bob!" She greeted him with warm pleasure. "Yes, I'm afraid Meg kept her word, and poor Sidney is feeling very sad."

"He'll get over it. You'll help him there, Kitty."

"Me?" She was surprised. "I don't think Sidney would ever expect help from me, Bob."

"Perhaps not now, but he will...in time." He broke off as her next partner came to claim her. "Don't forget that we have the supper dance!"

"I won't!" As she was swept away on to the floor Meg stopped beside her brother to ask why he was not dancing.

"My partner tore a flounce," he said. "And she is in the cloakroom having the damage repaired."

"Did I hear you say that you have the supper dance with Kitty?" asked Meg.

He looked down at her gravely. "Is there any reason why I shouldn't?"

"Well, only that I happen to know that you have had one dance with her already."

"What of it? I am having a third later on." His steady eyes dared her to find fault and she laughed.

"People will be saying you are in love with her," she accused him. "And Father is not going to like that at all! He may think she's too good for Mr. Burke—yes, he does, Bob! He told me so himself just now!—but I don't think he will consider her good enough for his only son!"

"Would you mind not talking quite so much nonsense?" said Bob gently.

"I adore Kitty, as you know," said Meg without heed-

119

ing him. "But I wouldn't like Mrs. Ralston as my mother in law!"

And then her partner took her away and Bob was free to go back to studying Kitty as she danced, her face animated, her eyes sparkling, Sidney's troubles forgotten in the joy of the moment, and he thought how sweet she was, little Kitty grown up, and what a fine person she was growing into. And although he was pretty certain that he was not falling in love with her, he was afraid that he might, given time and opportunity, and he thought it was a very good thing that she was leaving Belgrave Square on the following day.

On the afternoon after the ball Lady Winter was taking Meg and a party of young friends to a matinée, and when Kitty went to say goodbye to her after lunch, she tried to persuade her to go with them.

"We can easily send a telegram to your friends in Hampstead, dear," she said in her indolent way. "You can go to them tomorrow. We have a stage box, and there will be plenty of room for you."

Kitty said that Maidie was expecting her that afternoon. "And I told my mother I would be home tomorrow," she added. She asked if Lady Winter had heard any more about Daisy and the Suffragettes' march that afternoon, and she said she hadn't.

"It is tiresome enough for the Draytons to have Flora behaving so badly, without Daisy adding to it," she went on placidly. "But I daresay she will think better of it. You know, she will spoil her dress if she does go, and no girl likes to have her dresses torn and dirtied."

And then Meg came into the room, looking quite radiant in a new dress and picture hat, and she kissed Kitty fondly and said how terribly she was going to miss her, and that she must write to her every day, and she did not know how she was going to live without her, and she would come and see her in dear little White Cliff Bay as soon as she could find a week free from engagements. And then Grayson came to tell them that the motor car was at the door and she went without a backward glance.

Kitty watched from the window as the party of young people got into Sir Arthur's latest acquisition, Lady Winter preferring to travel more sedately in the carriage, as the wind blew her hair and hat about too much in the motor. It was still half an hour before a cab need be summoned to take her to Hampstead and left to herself, Kitty sat on the window seat overlooking the Square, thinking of the happy times she had had in this big house, and wishing that she had been able to say goodbye to Bob before she left. But Bob had gone out early that morning, and was lunching with his father at Sir Algernon Syme's club to discuss the Paris appointment. Kitty knew that it was to be an important meeting for Bob, but she wished she had more than the warm handshake and brief goodnight when they had parted in the small hours to remember. She was thinking about him when a cab drew up in front of the house and Sidney got out of it and a few minutes later was in the room.

"Kitty, my dear!" He hurried to her. "I've come with a message from Mother. Father had a heart attack in his dressing-room last night, and I have come to take you to Victoria instead of Hampstead in consequence. She sent her love and said that she knew you would understand."

"Why of course." Her first thought was of Wallie, and her next for Sidney, to whom his father's health meant so much. "Is he very bad?"

"Bad enough. I've looked up the trains, Kitty. There's one you can catch easily at three-thirty and another at half-past four."

"I'll go by the earlier one. And don't trouble to come with me, Sid. Go back to Aunt Maidie. I can manage by myself."

"No, I'll come. There's nothing I can do at home." Her luggage was put on the cab and they drove off. "We will ask the driver to go by Challoner Square," he said. "It is on the way to Victoria."

Kitty welcomed the idea. "Nobody seems the least worried about Daisy but you and me," she said.

"From what I hear," said Sidney, "old Drayton has washed his hands of his eldest daughter. Instead of looking on Flora as a martyr in a good cause he thinks she is nothing but a plaguey nuisance. I don't suppose he or Mrs. Drayton know that Daisy is to be with her this afternoon."

The attack on the Lord Chancellor's house had been advertised by pamphlets and slogans chalked on pavements in advance, and a small crowd had gathered on the north side of the square. As they arrived Kitty could see a line of police standing ready on the pavement outside the house, and their cabby refused to go any closer. He said he wasn't going to have his horse upset by a lot of blank women, and so Sidney left Kitty in the cab and got out to reconnoitre.

"Nothing has happened yet," he said when he returned, and Kitty's eyes followed his to the black vans standing on the pitch usually reserved for the cab stand under the plane trees, while at the same moment there came the sound of music and women's voices singing, and about a hundred women came marching down Challoner Road.

Their banners with "Votes for Women" on them were held steadily as they advanced like a besieging army on the Lord Chancellor's house, the only sign of life there being the frightened faces of women servants at the top windows. The police braced themselves for action, and no sooner had the marchers got within striking distance than they set about them.

"Devils!" cried Sidney, and Kitty jumped down beside him.

"I saw Daisy!" she said. "She was on the far side, holding a banner. Flora was in front of her."

"I think I can see Flora," Sidney said. "She's so large that you can't mistake her. A couple of bobbies are arguing with her. Now, Miss Drayton, be careful! Don't do anything unladylike...Oh, Lord, I was afraid of that!" Flora snatched off the helmet of the constable who was speaking to her and flung it into the Lord Chancellor's area, and at the same moment a volley of stones began splintering the windows above it. Kitty made a hasty movement and Sidney put out a restraining hand. "Hey, you aren't going to join them, are you, Sugar Mouse?"

"It's Daisy!" gasped Kitty. "I saw her fall...the woman behind her gave her a push I think, and she was hampered with that awful banner and fell...She's under all that crowd, Sid! They'll trample her to death."

"So they will, by George!" Sidney gripped her arm. "Get back into the cab and stay there, I'll see if I can get her out." He raced across the square to the struggling, screaming mob outside the Lord Chancellor's house, shouting at them as he came. "There's a girl being killed there! Can't you see what you are doing?"

Pushed and buffeted and hit by umbrellas and truncheons he forced his way to where Daisy was lying, and dragged her free of the melée and on to the pavement, where he was joined by Kitty, who had approached from the other side. She dropped on her knees beside her friend, exclaiming in horror at the sight of her cut and bleeding face.

"She's been hit by a stone!" she cried. "Is she unconscious, Sid?"

"It may be just a faint." He felt her pulse and made up his mind quickly. "I'm going to take her back to the Draytons' house in your cab, Kitty, and you'll have to catch the later train."

"Of course. I'll come with you."

At that moment a young constable arrived on the scene. "If that young woman's one of that lot she'd better go in the van along of the rest," he said wrathfully.

"She's only a schoolgirl," Sidney said shortly. "She was dragged into this by her sister, who is old enough to know better, and she's been hit on the head and nearly trampled to death by those fools of women. She may be badly hurt and I'm taking her home in that cab over there." He stooped over Daisy and raised her in his arms. "Help me to lift her, there's a good chap, and

123

handle her gently. Her ribs may be broken, and she's too young to bite you."

The young constable helped him to carry the unconscious girl across the square, his face concerned and crestfallen.

"I'm sorry the young lady's been hurt, sir," he said. "But it ain't our fault. These women come at you so...you've got to put 'em down somehow, haven't you?"

"They're going about it the wrong way," Sidney said. "They will never get the vote like this." They reached the cab and Kitty helped to settle Daisy on the seat and held her in her arms as they moved off: the light pretty dress she wore was dirty, torn and stained with blood.

"Lady Winter was right," Kitty said with a catch in her breath. "Poor Daisy has spoilt her clothes!"

It seemed an interminable drive to Manchester Square: every dray, horse, bus, hansom cab and four wheeler in London seemed to be making an effort to obstruct them, and when they arrived at last and Daisy was carried upstairs, it seemed an equally long time before Sidney came back to tell Kitty that the doctor and the girl's father had been sent for, and Mrs. Drayton had asked him to stay with her until they came. Mr. Drayton was the senior partner in a firm of stockbrokers in the City.

"Can you reach Victoria by yourself?" Sidney asked anxiously "I think I ought to stay with Mrs. Drayton."

"I wouldn't let you do anything else." She saw the relief in his face and smiled a little sadly. "I'm grown up now!" she reminded him, but she did not think he heard her. He hurried back into the house without waiting to see her go.

As the cab moved off she leaned back on the hard leather cushions conscious of arms that still trembled from holding Daisy, and scarcely seeing where she was being taken until the cab stopped at the bottom of Park Lane, waiting to turn into the traffic in Piccadilly. It was then that a young man waiting to cross the road saw her, and with an exclamation opened the door of her cab and jumped in beside her.

"Kitty!" cried Bob. "I thought you were going to Hampstead this afternoon? What has happened? Have you been in an accident?"

She glanced down at her white blouse where it was stained with Daisy's blood and hastily buttoned her jacket over it.

"No," she said. "At least...it was Daisy." A tear suddenly slid down her cheek and his hand came over the shaking ones clasped in her lap, and it was warm and comforting and strong.

"Tell me about it," he said gently and listened in silence to what she had to say, his face darkening with anger.

"But this is abominable!" he exclaimed when she had finished. "Do you mean to say that after such an experience Burke left you to go to Victoria on your own?"

"He felt he ought to stay with Mrs. Drayton," she explained.

"Why? Were there no servants to be with the lady until the doctor came? But you were not even asked inside the front door, and neither was a maid sent for to wash the stains from that pretty blouse."

"Don't...Please Bob dear, don't! It doesn't matter."

"But it does matter!" He took his hand away and folded his arms, sitting stiff and furious in his corner of the cab. "When I see Burke again and I shall tell him exactly what I think of him!"

At Victoria he paid off the cabby, bought her ticket, saw the luggage into the van and herself into a first-class compartment labelled Ladies Only, first assuring himself that the two ladies in it were travelling to White Cliff Bay, and tipped the guard to keep an eye on her, as if, she thought, amused and touched by his care of her, she was twelve years old.

And when her train finally drew out of the station she knew that it was only Bob with whom she would part with heartache and the deep, hot feeling of unshed tears. The luxury of the big house in Belgrave Square meant nothing to her any more; it had only been a bait tempting her to live for a time in Meg's artificial world, in which she had no real part.

Bob alone had been real: Bob, to whom the chivalrous care of women came as second nature, to whom right was right and wrong was wrong, and the lack of manners in a man were almost worse than a lack of morals. Bob, who would be her very perfect, gentle knight until the day she died....

13

At Cranston Stephen Brett received his brother-in-law with even less enthusiasm than usual. Muriel was expecting her fifth child and things were not going well with her. A London specialist had been called in to consult with their own doctor and the opinion of both had been that if the child's life was to be saved the mother must rest continually until it was born.

"There was no trouble with the others," Stephen said resentfully. "At least, I believe you were a little worried about the last baby, Dr. Starr, but as things turned out, without any reason."

"It was a breach case," said the doctor stiffly. "Your wife was three days in labour. She is small boned and delicately made, Mr. Brett, and not an easy person to deliver of a child in any case. But she was so exhausted on that occasion that I warned you it might be wise to wait a few years before having any more additions to your family."

Stephen glared at him in silence. Muriel had been a disappointment to him over her children: four girls was not a good record when a man wanted an heir. All he could do was to hope that it would be a boy this time, and if Dr. Starr could have guaranteed this he would have forgiven him for his unsolicited criticism and advice.

Muriel laughed at the doctor's fears. "Don't worry so much, darling!" she told her husband. "You'll have your boy this time." And she went off to play with the little girls in the nursery as happily as if she could supply him with four boys at any given moment. Her mother however put a new fear into his mind.

"I'm afraid dear Muriel is not as strong as we could wish her to be, Stephen," she said. "We must take great care of her. It would be too dreadful if the darling girl were to be an invalid for the rest of her life."

An invalid wife, with a nursery full of girls... Stephen's mind was still dwelling on the unwelcome prospect when Richard came to dinner. At first he did not pay any attention to the description the young man was giving Muriel of Meg Winter's coming-out ball, and then, while they were at dessert, a name caught his attention and he stiffened.

"I beg your pardon?" He stared at his brother-in-law incredulously.

"I was talking about Meg's little school-friend, Kitty Ralston," said Richard pleasantly. He saw the silver fruit knife in Stephen's hand stop in the task of peeling a peach for his wife, and went on: "Her father was killed in the South African War, or so I have been told. I often wondered if she could be related to you, Stephen, with that name?"

Stephen Brett finished peeling the peach with care before handing it to his wife and saying coldly, "I should hardly think so. Although Ralston was the name of my mother's family, it is not uncommon."

Muriel said she did not think she wanted the peach after all: it was not very sweet. She dipped her fingers daintily in her finger bowl, and left the room with her mother for the south drawing-room, which was her favourite room.

128

"Help yourself to port," said Stephen when the butler had put the wine in front of them and the servants had left the room. Richard did so, and as he passed the decanter back to his brother-in-law he said thoughtfully:

"It's a strange thing but ever since I was staying in White Cliff Bay last summer and met Miss Ralston's mother there, I have had my doubts about her husband. I understand that there are no portraits of Mr. Ralston in the house, and the man's portrait is not the only thing that is missing in his family. He himself is missing, too. He is never mentioned in conversation, which is curious, because Mrs. Ralston is the kind of woman one would expect to refer to the late lamented constantly. You know the sort of thing, I'm sure... 'My dear husband was so good at golf'... or 'so fond of turbot'... 'My dear husband was such a handsome man. Kitty is so like him.' But there is nothing... nothing at all. The man is such a nonentity in fact that one begins to wonder if he ever existed."

"Perhaps they did not get on well together," said Stephen but Richard was pleased to observe the uneasiness in his eyes.

"Or on the other hand he may have done something disgraceful," pursued Richard smiling. "Was he by any chance, the one black sheep in your mother's family?"

"I have already told you that he was nothing to do with the Ralstons." But Stephen was beginning to wear a hunted look, and Richard pressed home his advantage.

"No, but he was something to do with you, wasn't he?"

Brett caught his breath. "You impudent young devil!" he choked. "What the deuce do you mean?"

"When I said there were no photographs of Mr. Ralston at Flint House I meant there were none visible. The only one was hidden away and treasured by Ralston's daughter, Kitty. I saw it in the gold locket she was wearing on the night of Meg's ball."

"Oh, my God!" The exclamation slipped out before

129

Brett could stop it and Richard sipped his port and watched his brother-in-law's agitated face with cool interest. "Why have you told me this?" asked Stephen after a moment, pushing his wine glass away. "What do you want?" And then more anxiously, "You haven't told your sister?"

"No, and I've no intention of telling her, as long as you behave yourself. As you know I sail for India in a few weeks' time, and I went to see my mother's lawyer before coming here, and made certain arrangements on her behalf. He is drawing up an agreement for you to sign before I leave, by which she becomes tenant of the Dower House for the next seven years, with an option of renewal at the end of that time. I'm having no more of this 'grace and favour' business where she is concerned. As her landlord you will also do repairs long over-due. The roof leaks like a sieve, the kitchen needs a new range, the whole house needs painting and decorating, the garden should have a couple of gardeners, which she cannot afford on her income. You will put these things in hand at once, and you will undertake to pay the wages of the gardeners and all other servants needed by her over and above old Eliza. As you turned Mother out of Ivy Lodge for her sister, Mrs. Cartwright, I feel that you owe her some sort of compensation." He pushed back his chair.

"Of course I will sign anything you want me to sign if it will make your mother comfortable at the Dower House," Stephen said hurriedly. "I'm afraid I have not been as considerate to her as I might have been. But I will give you an undertaking to do all I can for her while you are away, Richard, and I will look after her for you. There I give you my word. But you must believe me when I say that I put an end to the affair with...Effie Fotheringay...before I asked your sister to marry me, and I have never given a thought to her since."

Richard's dislike for his brother-in-law increased as he glanced contemptuously at his stricken face. "People don't mean much to you, do they?" he said, and left him to his port.

He went into the south drawing-room and found his sister there with her head bent over a cushion cover, which she was embroidering with tiny, beautiful stitches. She put it down with a smile as he entered and made room for him on the settee beside her.

"Mother is paying her nightly visit to Nannie in the nursery," she said. "She adores gossiping with her about the children. How was London when you left it today?"

"So hot and dusty that I was afraid that Cartwright might have fled from it, too."

Muriel laughed. "Now then, Ricky! Sophie is really a very nice woman under it all."

"Under all that spitefulness, do you mean?"

"She doesn't mean to be spiteful, darling!"

"My dearest sister, how can people be spiteful without meaning to be? Sophie means to be spiteful, just as she meant to turn Mother out of her cozy little house." He laughed at her teasingly. "Even your pure mind can't refute that."

She stopped smiling for a moment. "Rick," she said gently, putting her hand on his knee. "Don't talk about those...Ralstons while you are here. Stephen doesn't like it."

"Doesn't he indeed?" He tried to laugh it off. "Then I won't mention them in future."

She picked up the cushion cover and put in a tiny green stitch. "You see dear," she said quietly, "I know who Stephen Ralston was...or is, rather, because he is still alive."

"Muriel!" He gave a stifled exclamation. "You *know*?"

"Yes, dear. I've known for quite a long time."

"But..." He was bewildered by her calm manner. "When did you find out?"

She shrugged her shoulders. "One heard rumours from Sophie and others. And then one day I was looking through some old photograph albums in a cupboard in the library and I came across a newspaper that had been stuffed down behind them. There was an address pencilled at the top, 'No. 47, Willowbrook Road,' and

I remembered seeing it written on a telegram that Stephen had been sending one day from the post office here, to inform a Mrs. Ralston there that her husband had been killed in South Africa. I unfolded the paper expecting to find the name in the casualty lists, but there was nothing except a message scribbled in the margin."

"A message?"

"Yes. I forget the wording, because I destroyed the paper, but it said that somebody was waiting for a telegram, which seemed odd." Muriel paused and threaded another needle with pink. "When we went to London that autumn I took a cab out to Willowbrook Road one morning while Stephen was busy with his lawyer, and I called at the next door house to No. 47 and told the lady there that I was making some enquiries about some old friends of mine called Ralston, who used to live there. Did she know what had happened to them? She was a very nice woman, and she said that Mr. Ralston had been killed in South Africa, and that his widow and children had moved to the South Coast, but she did not know where they were now as she had not kept up with them. So I said, 'I wonder if we are speaking of the same people? This is the Mr. Ralston that I knew,' and I showed her a photograph of Stephen, and she said at once, oh, yes, that was Mr. Ralston, and it was an excellent likeness...And then I was quite sure." She snipped off the pink silk and smiled affectionately at her brother.

"And you didn't...*mind*?" he asked, feeling that the comprehension of women was beyond him.

"Why should I mind?" She patted his hand. "It was over long before I married Stephen, and from what I've been able to discover since the woman was nobody of any importance...I think she was an actress, or something of the sort. The whole affair was of no consequence whatever."

Effie was far more interested in Meg's coming-out ball than in what happened to Daisy.

"Serves her right for being such a little fool," she said contemptuously. "But I'm sorry Wallie is ill. It is a pity Sidney didn't let you know sooner, then you could have stayed on with the Winters for another week."

"I couldn't do that, Mother. I was only asked for the ball."

"Pooh, I wouldn't have given that a thought if I'd been you. You want to take all the chances you can get, my girl. What did Lady Winter think of your dress? It cost me a pretty penny, I can tell you. Did you dance every dance, and did any nice young man propose to you?"

"Mother!" Kitty laughed. "As if any one would be likely to on so short an acquaintance!"

"I don't see why not. You are pretty enough. I'd hoped you might get Bob Winter up to scratch."

Kitty coloured up. "Bob won't think of marrying anybody for years," she said quickly. "He's got his career to think about. Lady Winter said so."

Effie brushed this aside impatiently. "Lady Winter was warning you off the turf, my dear," she said with a frankness that made her daughter wince. "His career wouldn't matter a sixpence to a young man like Bob if he wanted to marry a lord's daughter. But Lady Winter doesn't want a little nobody for a daughter-in-law." She eyed Kitty discontentedly. "I don't know why I sent you to that high-class school. You seem to miss your best opportunities through sheer stupidity."

Kitty stiffened, wondering if her mother knew how deeply her words hurt. "I can't believe that you only sent me to Miss Westlake's so that I could get a rich husband through one of the girls there!" she said as lightly as she could.

"And where's the harm in that?" Effie's voice was suddenly shrill. "You needn't think there'll be rich young men dancing attendance on you down here, because there won't. You may have been taken up by the Winters in London, but nobody is going to bother about you in White Cliff Bay. If I'd had half your chances at your age and a young man like Bob making sheep's eyes at me he'd not have escaped me as he has you. I'd have got my hands so firmly on to him by this time that only a breach of promise would have freed him."

Kitty went off for a walk up the headland to get the bad taste of her mother's words out of her mind. She wondered, as she climbed to the top, if Lady Winter really had been warning her off, as Effie put it, and if it had occurred to Bob to think that she might have made friends with Meg in order to catch her brother. But Bob's clear eyes saw through shams, and she did not think he would have treated her so kindly if he had thought anything of the sort.

It was ten days later that the blow fell. The morning post had come and among the letters was a square envelope with a London postmark, addressed to Mrs. Ralston in a fine copper-plate hand.

"Old Fanshawe writing about something," said Effie. She glanced through the other letters, saying that they were only bills, and then she opened the lawyer's letter. As she read it she gave an exclamation of dismay and anger and her face went first white and then red.

"I don't believe it!" she gasped. "The mean, dirty so-and-so.... After all these years!"

"Mother." Kitty went to her in alarm. "What is it? What has happened?"

"I've done nothing to warrant such treatment!" said Effie indignantly. "I've kept out of his way...I don't know what he means by it." Her eyes filled with angry tears.

Kitty became frightened. "What is the matter?" she asked again. "Mother darling, don't cry...just tell me."

"Oh, read it for yourself!" Effie threw the letter on to the table. "It's plain enough."

Kitty picked up the lawyer's letter and read:

"*Madam,*
Our client, Mr. Stephen Ralston Brett, has instructed us to cancel your allowance forthwith, as it was paid to you on the understanding that you would not annoy or molest him in any way. This condition, he maintains,
134

has not lately been adhered to, and he therefore dis-
claims all further responsibility in the matter.
　　　　　Yours faithfully,
　　　　　Fanshawe, Fanshawe and Creditor."

"Mr. Stephen Ralston Brett." Kitty repeated the
name slowly. "But I don't understand. Has he been
giving us an allowance then since Father was killed?"

"It might have been Meg's ball. Somebody might
have been there, who knew who you were." Effie dashed
away her tears and looked at her daughter suspiciously.
"Can you remember any stranger asking to be introduced to you?"

"But there were dozens...all friends of the Winters.
I don't remember half their names...I couldn't if I
tried."

"And that Lestrange boy...Did you dance with
him?"

"Of course," Kitty suddenly remembered the little
episode of the locket and the expression on Richard's
face as he recognised the photograph inside it. "Mother,"
she said slowly, "did Father do anything to make his
family ashamed of him? I mean, did he go to prison, or
anything like that?"

"Go to prison? Whatever put that idea into your
head?" Effie was impatient.

"Only the way that Richard looked when I showed
him my locket."

"Your locket?" Effie looked up sharply. "What do you
mean? Out with it, my girl. What is all this about a
locket?"

"It was that gold locket that Meg gave me. I showed
it to you." Kitty spoke humbly, aware that she had
done wrong but not seeing that it could have serious
consequences. "It was exactly the right size to take
Father's head from that old photograph that was
thrown on the bonfire when we left Willowbrook Road.
Sidney saved it for me and I kept it. I stood it on my
dressing table at school, and Meg knew you wouldn't
like me to have it when I came home, and so she gave
135

me the locket and I cut Father's face from the photograph and fitted it inside. But nobody could see it unless I opened the locket to show them."

"And you showed it to young Lestrange?" Effie spoke with dangerous calm.

"Yes, but why shouldn't I?" Kitty's voice rose desperately. "Mother, what is all this mystery about Father?"

Effie ignored the question. "It is easy now to see what happened," she said. "Lestrange went straight back to Cranston and told Stephen about you being Meg Winter's friend. I never liked that young man: he was stuck up and supercilious and impertinent, and much too inquisitive. I could see that he suspected something at that stupid picnic last year." She stared at Kitty angrily. "Cal said it would have to come out sooner or later, and it has."

"What had to come out?" The apprehension was growing in Kitty's heart.

"Why, that you and Johnnie are Stephen Brett's children. The story about him going to South Africa and getting killed was poppy cock: I invented it for the sake of our friends, and the servants and Miss Childs. Don't stare at me like that. You are old enough now to know these things."

"But...did you divorce him?" The unbending attitude of Lady Winter and her friends towards divorce swam into Kitty's mind and dizzily swam out again.

"Why on earth should I do that, when I wasn't even married to him?"

Mother and daughter looked at each other across the room, the mother with genuine surprise, the daughter with horror. Such a possibility had never entered Kitty's head, and at first she could not take it in, but Effie was too absorbed in her anger with Stephen to consider the effect of her information. The resentment that had been building up for years against Stephen took possession of her, and she began pacing up and down the room, her hands gripping each other, her eyes dark with rage.

"I'll get my own back on him," she said. "He'll be sorry he ever crossed my path by the time I've finished with him. And I'll go back to the stage at once. Cal is back in London and he will help me. He'll look after me."

"Mother..." Kitty tried to find a foothold in the quicksands of Effie's fury. "*Please* don't! Please let us try to think it out calmly by ourselves. I'm sure we can manage without the money...and without Mr. Ricketts's help. We've got each other."

Effie glanced at her strangely. "We've got each other!" she mocked her. "No, my dear, this has freed me from you and Johnnie. You can go back to your father now."

"But that is impossible!" Kitty stiffened into revolt. "Johnnie must not know about this...at least, not yet. He has always looked up to Father...as I have. He's been a hero to us really." Her young voice faltered and Effie laughed. "Yes, you may laugh," said Kitty passionately. "But it is true....It would be a dreadful shock to Johnnie to discover now that Father was...the sort of man who had tricked you into thinking that he could not marry you."

"Tricked me? Nobody tricked *me*, I assure you, my dear! I knew exactly what I was doing when...I took up with Steve. But he was very rich, and he said he was in love with me, and he promised me the world..." But he had not promised marriage, and seeing that her mother had forgotten her Kitty went up to her room and sat there for a long time, looking down at the empty beach in front of the house.

Whatever might be the outcome of it all one thing was clear: she and Johnnie were now enclosed by circumstances in a prison from which there was no escape. They would never be able to meet any of their acquaintances in the town without a feeling of shame, of being apart, of being outside the pale, and the isolation of their position cut her to the quick, so that at last she put her head down on her arms and wept.

Wept for Sidney and his companionship that Meg

had stolen from her, wept for Meg and for that dear, chivalrous Bob who was lost to her, and wept for the false image of a dead hero that she had carried with her over five loyal years....

14

During the days that followed Effie refused to discuss her affairs with her daughter: whenever she tried to talk to her about their future she laughed and said that something would turn up, but Kitty had the uneasy feeling that the course she intended to take was already set in her mind.

One morning towards the end of July she told Kitty that she had met Miss Grant in the town and she had asked them to go to St. David's that afternoon for the last big cricket match of the term.

"As Johnnie is Captain of the Eleven I suppose she thought we would be delighted to go," she said. "I told her that cricket bored me, and I could not sit through an hour of it, even if my only son knocked up a century, but that you would go and clap his runs for me."

"I would love to." Even a school cricket match would relieve the uneasy tension of the past days.

"You need not hurry home," added Effie lightly. "Miss Grant wants you to stay to tea."

The cricket pitch at St. David's was surrounded by

tall trees, under which seats and wickerwork chairs were placed for the visitors, the turf smooth and green in contrast to the youthful figures in white flannels who batted and bowled and fielded there. For a few hours Kitty was able to forget the problems that faced her at home and to concentrate on the game instead.

It was past seven o'clock by the time she got home, and found Clara waiting for her, her face charged with drama.

"Your ma's gorn!" she said.

"You mean that she's gone out to tea?" asked Kitty, surprised.

"No, she ain't then. She's gorn to London," said Clara with ghoulish relish. "Not that I'm surprised, mind you, with her packing her clothes as she's been doing the last few days."

"Packing her clothes?" Kitty sat down on the hall chair, remembering how she had been excluded from her mother's room. "When did she go?"

"Soon after you'd gorn to the cricket match. The station cab came—she must hev ordered it when she was out this morning—and she calls the cabby to bring her luggage down the stairs. Several trunks there was: she's left nothing but a few old dresses be'ind 'er. Then down she comes in 'er best 'at and fevver boa, buttoning her gloves. 'Clara,' says she, 'I'm goin' to London and I'm not sure when I'll be back. I've left a note for Miss Kitty.' And off she goes, wavin' 'er 'and and looking as pleased as Punch."

An envelope addressed to her in her mother's writing was on the hall-table, and as Kitty opened it four five pound notes fell out into her lap.

"*My dear Kitty,*" Effie wrote. "*I am joining Calverley in London and when he leaves for his American tour next month I shall go with him. The enclosed is all that remains of my last quarter's allowance, and if you run short of cash I suggest that you sell the furniture, or apply to your friends the Winters for assistance. E. Ralston.*"

140

Not a word of affection, not a thought of apology or regret.

"She 'as gorn, 'asn't she?" said Clara, who had been watching her perusal of the letter with interest.

"Yes," Kitty tried to pull herself together.

"I thought she 'ad." Clara nodded wisely. "So you've been deserted by both your Pa and Ma now, 'ave you, dear?"

Kitty looked at her quickly. "How did you know about...my father?" she asked.

"Oh, I used to 'ear your Ma and Mr. Ricketts talking. They never troubled to lower their voices when I was about. I dessay they thought I was deaf. But I ain't deaf, and I ain't a fool, and I can put two and two together well as most." She put a rheumatic hand on the girl's arm with rough kindliness. "Don't you fret, my dear. We'll manage between us."

But on what, Kitty thought, staring at the notes in her lap, and for how long? It was a thought that was to keep her awake for many nights to come.

In the morning, sitting at Effie's pretty little desk in the drawing-room, twenty pounds seemed to be quite a lot of money, but by the time Kitty had added up the totals in the tradesmen's books, and discovered that Clara's wages had not been paid since April, and that there was a dressmaker's bill outstanding of one hundred and fifty pounds, to which her own ball-dress had contributed ten, she began to realise that she really had nothing at all. She decided to pay the old servant and settle the weekly books, and to pay five pounds off the dress account, but in this she was stopped by Clara.

"Ladies like your Ma is used to running up dress-bills," she said. "The dressmaker won't think nothing of being kept waiting. But if you goes and pays five pounds off of a bill this size she'll smell a rat and want the lot. So I'd put it on one side and forget about it for a time, if I was you."

Kitty saw the sense in this, although she felt it to be dishonest, and she put the bill away in one of the desk's pigeonholes and began to discuss with Clara how they could cut down on the food when Johnnie came home.

"I know chickens only cost a shilling or two, Clara," she said, trying to curb the old woman's desire to give them something fancy. "But if Mother doesn't send me any more money it is just that shilling or two too much. And we will do without cream on our Sunday apple pie."

An obstinate look appeared on Clara's face. "Master Johnnie is a growing lad and needs feeding up," she said sourly.

"We must feed him up on stews and bread and jam then," said Kitty. "Joints of meat cost money. That leg of mutton the butcher sent last week was three shillings and sixpence."

"But it was the best English mutton!" Clara was indignant. "And you've always had the best, Miss Kitty. Your Ma wouldn't 'ave a cheap cut of meat in the 'ouse."

"But we must have cheap cuts in the future." Kitty was firm. "Scrag end makes a good stew, Clara, and it's only a few pence a pound. Oh, and I saw in the baker's window that if you went round to the back of the shop on Saturday nights you could have as much of the day's bread as you could carry for sixpence."

"Scrag end and stale bread!" said Clara, scandalised. "Whatever next? You'll be saying you won't 'ave a negg for your breakfast soon."

"I'm getting tired of eggs," agreed Kitty. "I'd rather have bread and marmalade and keep the eggs for when Johnnie is home."

That week she heard from Sidney, a short, scrappy letter in which he told her that his father had recovered, and that her friend Daisy was a great deal better, too.

"*She got off lightly as it happened,*" he wrote. "*Concussion and a couple of cracked ribs were the most serious injuries. I was asked to dinner last week to celebrate her recovery, and Mrs. Drayton asked to be remembered to you. Her gratitude is out of all proportion*
142

to what we did for poor Daisy that day. I understand that Flora is once more residing in Holloway." And then in a postscript: "*I saw Bob Winter one day last week and he cut me dead. What an objectionable fellow he is!*"

A few days before Johnnie came home from school Kitty found Daisy waiting for her in the drawing-room when she came in.

"Kitty, my dear!" Daisy jumped up and kissed her affectionately. "How lovely to see you again, and what a funny old house you live in! I'd no idea it was like this." She looked about her smilingly and Kitty was able to admire the new frilly hat, the muslin dress and the lace-edged parasol, and thought how grown-up and pretty Daisy had become.

"Are you staying here?" she asked as they sat down together on the window-seat overlooking the sea.

"Just for a few days at the Marine Hotel. Mammā has taken a suite of rooms there until we go on to Eastbourne." Daisy was full of her own concerns. "Father called in Sir Mostyn Craig because he didn't think I was getting on as well as I should, and he suggested that I should have a few weeks of bracing sea air. So, because Mamma wanted to thank you herself for what you did for me that awful day, she thought it would be nice if we came to White Cliff Bay first."

Kitty said she was delighted, but that no thanks were needed. "It was Mr. Burke who did it all," she added.

"Oh, Mr. Burke has been an angel!" Daisy cried. "He has been to dinner several times since I have been downstairs, and Father thinks he is a very clever young man. He told him that he ought to become a consultant, like Sir Mostyn, and he said he would think about it."

But Sidney had often told her that only rich men's sons could afford to specialise in medicine, and when she went to tea with Mrs. Drayton in her private sitting-room at the hotel that afternoon, and had to listen to the lady's eulogies of Mr. Burke, too, she began to wonder if Daisy's helpless air and fragile daintiness had made an equal impression on him, and if the thought has occurred to him that with a rich wife, specialising in medicine would not be so very far away after all.

"This silly little girl of mine has a new craze now," Mrs. Drayton told Kitty fondly. "She wants to be a nurse! So I asked Mr. Burke to tell her what a nurse's life is like, and I think he almost persuaded her to change her mind, didn't he, my pet?"

Daisy laughed. "He did paint it in rather gloomy colours," she admitted ruefully.

"Only four hours off duty a week," her mother reminded her playfully. "Disgusting food to eat, and sleeping in a dormitory in an attic of the hospital with a lot of other girls... No dances, or theatre visits, or anything like that."

"I wouldn't mind all that," Daisy said plaintively, "as long as the Ward Sister didn't bully me. The nurse Sir Mostyn got for me said that some of them are simply dreadful, but Mr. Burke said that was because most of the Ward Sisters are middle-aged women who have spent their working lives in charge of the same ward, and that everybody adores them and thinks they are wonderful really, under all their starch and discipline."

Kitty laughed. "At all events if you were a nurse you wouldn't have time to go marching with the Suffragettes again!" she said teasingly.

"No." Daisy looked a little self-conscious. "I don't think I was ever meant to be one of the heroines of the Women's Suffrage Movement!" After a moment she went on, "Violet says that the nearest I'll ever get to *nursing* will be if I were to marry a doctor! But I said 'Why not?' I think some doctors are very charming people."

"Anyway she will have to wait until she is twenty-three before they will accept her for training at any hospital," Mrs. Drayton said comfortably. "So I daresay she will have found much more absorbing interests by then!" It was the desire of her life to get her daughters married, and although Flora had been a big disappointment she did not see why Violet and Daisy should not do as she wished.

In the meantime Kitty was glad that Mrs. Drayton felt that mornings spent on the beach and afternoons out driving in her motor-car were better for her invalid than frequent visits to her old school-friend: it hurt a little to discover how much Daisy had been seeing of Sidney. It seemed that Mr. Burke had ample time to give to new friends, where he could not spare a thought for the old.

On the day that the Draytons left Johnnie came home, and that evening Kitty took him on to the empty beach in front of Flint House and told him about their father, and how Effie had added her desertion to his. She felt that he must know the truth, young as he was, and to her surprise he took the whole thing with calm cheerfulness.

"I thought something like that had happened," he said. "About Father I mean. Mother would never talk about him, you see."

"Then you don't mind being...being..."

"A bastard?" he finished for her with a comical look. "No, I don't, and I hope you don't either. It makes no difference to us, does it? I'm still me, and you are you, and it's a good thing to know where we stand."

"Yes, but now that both our parents have washed their hands of us, Johnnie dear, I don't quite know what we are to do for an income."

He gave her hand a comforting squeeze. "One thing seems clear at any rate. I must finish with school, and hooray for that, says I!"

"Oh, Johnnie!" Her voice shook. "You shouldn't have finished. You have still so much to learn. And what can you do at your age?"

"Earn some money. At the worst I'll go as errand boy to Mr. Fry. He pays his boys five shillings a week."

"No, but seriously, Johnnie, what are we to do?"

He thought it over and then he suggested going to see Mr. Grant. "He's an awfully decent old chap, Kit, and I'm sure he would help us."

It was only a straw, but Kitty was in the mood to catch at straws, and the next morning she went with her brother to see the schoolmaster. They told him everything, laying before him their problem of how to exist, and as he met their grave young eyes and realised from his wider experience the pitfalls that must lay in front of them, he felt he would have liked to strangle their heartless mother.

"Johnnie is right of course," he said quietly. "As there are no longer any funds from which to pay school fees he should start earning at once, and I believe I might be able to help there. Mr. Webber needs a new office boy, and I think if I spoke to him he might be prepared to take him on. Mind you the salary would not be princely, but if it was no more than Mr. Fry's five shillings at least it would be an improvement on going round in the cart with legs of mutton."

After they had left, much encouraged by his interest and kindness, he told his sister what he felt she should know about the situation, and Miss Grant could not hide her astonishment at hearing that eighteen-year-old Kitty and her brother were alone at Flint House. Why, she asked, had not Mrs. Ralston taken them with her to London?

"Without going into that," said her brother. "I was wondering if you could not use Miss Kitty's services in your little school? You were complaining yesterday that you had not enough young ladies to help with your charges in the holidays. Why not employ her then? It will help her and you."

Miss Grant protested that Kitty was too young and knew nothing about children. She had been sent by her silly mother to a school full of the daughters of wealthy people and would have ideas far above her station. But in the end her brother prevailed on her to give her a trial at a weekly wage of fifteen shillings and her mid-day dinner.

"But only for the holidays, mind!" she added. "When my regular governesses return in September she will go."

An appointment was made for them with Mr. Webber, and the lawyer, whom they remembered as a genial host at the Christmas parties, subjected them to sharp scrutiny.

Why did Johnnie want to start work at his age? he asked. Most boys from St. David's went on to a public school and then the 'varsity.

"Excuse me, sir, but I can't go to a public school or the 'varsity when I've no money," pointed out Johnnie.

"But Mr. Grant says your father is still alive. Won't he pay?"

There was a short silence in the office and then Kitty said quietly: "Mr. Webber, Johnnie and I have no legal claim on our father. He was not married to our mother."

"I see." The lawyer pressed the tips of his fingers together and surveyed the young people thoughtfully. "He could be approached for money, all the same, and in fact, persuaded to contribute to your support. But perhaps you don't wish for that?"

"On no account..."

"Oh, no, sir!" Brother and sister spoke together and the lawyer allowed himself a frosty smile.

"You may be wise to take that attitude: it can be humiliating to force favours of that kind." His smile grew less frosty. "But if you come to work for me, John, I cannot pay you more than seven shillings and sixpence a week, and out of that there is your food to find, and you will need a suit of dark clothes. You cannot work in an office like mine in a Norfolk suit."

"If you engage my brother, Mr. Webber," Kitty said steadily, "he shall have all the clothes he needs, and Miss Grant has given me a holiday post in her little school, so that we shall make out between us very well."

"I see." Rather uncomfortably she felt that Mr. Webber's sharp eyes saw a great deal more than she had intended. "Well, John, Mr. Grant's report on your work encourages me to engage you, starting next Monday morning. The hours are from nine in the morning until six at night, with half an hour off for your dinner in the middle of the day. And remember...a dark suit!"

147

They promised that it should be obtained and left the office treading on air, and went at once to see the tailor, Mr. Bent, in Fish Lane, who clicked his tongue over the inches Johnnie had grown since he last measured him, and promised that they should have the suit by Saturday night.

"I will deliver it at Flint House personally," he said. "I know Mr. Webber. Very particular gentleman he is, but fair and just. You are fortunate to be starting your career in his office, my dear young sir."

The price agreed upon for the new suit was thirty shillings and as they walked on up the lane to the sea front Johnnie asked his sister if she had that amount of money.

"Not yet," she said smiling. "But I shall have it by Saturday night."

That evening after Johnnie was in bed she gave Clara notice, but the old woman flatly refused to leave them.

"I don't want no wages," she said angrily. "And I don't eat much at my age. I can't and won't leave you two young creatures along 'ere in this big 'ouse on your own. You might be murdered in your beds."

Although Kitty could have laughed at the thought of Clara being a protection against murderers, she nearly cried too at her goodness of heart, and compromised by giving her a silent hug. In the morning she paid a visit to the jeweller's in the High Street.

"Mr. Ponting," she said with more boldness than she felt, "I've got a little trinket to sell, and I wondered if you would like to buy it from me?"

"Depends on what you want for it, my dear." Mr. Ponting took Meg's locket from her and examined it under his glass and his manner subtly changed. "This is a very beautiful little locket, but I'm not a pawnbroker. I can't lend money on it, I'm afraid."

"No. I didn't think you would. That is why I want to sell it."

"Are you sure? It is quite valuable."

"I know."

148

"And how much do you want for it then?"

"Thirty shillings, I can't take any less."

"And I would not offer you less, because it is worth a great deal more than that." He rubbed his nose thoughtfully. "If I buy it from you I don't know when I should sell it again, because I don't do a lot of trade in good jewellery you see. Most of it is bead necklaces, and imitation pearls, and five shilling watches and rolled-gold brooches and the like. But I will give you thirty shillings for it gladly, and if I get any more than that when I sell it, I will halve it with you. I can't speak fairer than that, can I?"

The locket lay on the black velvet cloth on his counter and she saw in it the house in Belgrave Square, the servants and the carriages, the new motor-car. She heard Meg's laughter and saw her charming, exasperating face, and she saw Bob, and heard the deep, concerned tones of his voice, and she bit her lip to stop it from trembling, and drew a deep breath to stop the tears from forcing their way to her eyes.

"No," she said slowly. "You can't say fairer than that, Mr. Ponting. I'll take the thirty shillings now."

He put the gold sovereign and four half-crowns into her hand, and she put them away in her purse and went home, feeling that she had left her heart behind her, close shut up in the locket, on Mr. Ponting's counter.

15

Every Saturday night Kitty and her brother put their money down on the table in the little morning-room and compared it with the household books, and put what was over towards the dressmaker's bill, and it was not until Kitty's temporary employment with Miss Grant ended that things began to assume a less rosy aspect.

At first she was sure that she would get something to do very quickly, but although she advertised in the local paper and put a notice in the newsagent's window for a daily post as nursery governess to young children, nobody seemed to require her services.

"I wish I was older and could earn more money," sighed Johnnie. "The head clerk in Mr. Webber's office is getting two hundred pounds a year! If I were earning that there would be no need for you to go out and work, would there, Kit?"

"But I like earning my keep!" she assured him smiling, and it was only after another two weeks of fruitless search that she began to think seriously about selling the furniture. When she approached the furniture dealer in Fish Lane, however, he scratched his bald head, settled his steel-rimmed spectacles on his nose, and said it was not in his line of business at all.

"You see, I only buys old rubbish and sets to work on it and mends the inlay and polishes it up and sells it for a bit more than what I give. That's my trade. I don't deal in high class stuff." He saw the disappointment in her face and added, "But I knows a firm in Brighton that does, though you want to fix your price high. They'll beat you down if they can."

She wrote to the firm and a bland gentleman arrived one morning, notebook in hand, and bid so little for the dining-room suite that she refused it indignantly.

"The table is solid mahogany," she protested. "And it has three leaves in it. You'd have to pay ten pounds for a table like that new." So much she had gleaned from Clara.

"Ah, yes, I daresay you would, my dear. But it isn't new and you aren't buying the table. You are selling it." The gentleman became even more bland, smiled in a superior way and put his note-book away. "I'll give you ten pound for the lot," he said sharply. "Sideboard, table, chairs and two fireside arm-chairs, and I'm a fool to do it. But I will pay cash for it, and I will send a van to collect it on Monday morning."

As it was an advance on his first offer she accepted it in case he changed his mind, and he counted the ten sovereigns out on the table. She put two pounds towards the dress bill and the rest kept them until the middle of December, when she was forced to summon the bland gentleman again.

Clara closed the rooms as they were emptied of their contents, because once the bland gentleman got his foot into Flint House there was no stopping him. The drawing-room furniture went for a song, the stair carpets were ruthlessly pulled up and despatched with the hall rugs and pictures, and Kitty and her brother moved into two small dressing-rooms on the first floor, using the little morning as a living and dining-room, because they could manage there on mild evenings without a fire. Clara kept the curtains up throughout the house because the salt air had rotted and faded them so much that they would not have fetched a penny.

One Saturday afternoon before Christmas Johnnie had bundled up some driftwood on the shore to take home with him when he was stopped by a friendly fisherman.

"You've no call to take that, sonny," he said. "All driftwood hereabouts belongs to the lady of the manor. She makes a tidy sum out of it, which she gives to seamen's charities."

"I'm sorry. I thought everything on the beach was free." Johnnie let go his bundle with a chagrined air. "Who is the lady of the manor?"

"Old Lady Winter up at The Gables." The man glanced at him curiously. "Do you want the wood for boat-building?"

"No," said Johnnie bluntly. "For firing."

"For firing?" The man's surprise showed in his face. "But haven't you any coal then?"

"Only for the kitchen fire, and that's one and fourpence a hundredweight. We used to sit with our coats on and creep down to the kitchen after Clara was in bed, but now she rakes out the ash overnight to save fuel." He smiled cheerfully at the man's shocked expression. "We'll have to go on wearing our coats, that's all!"

"No...wait a bit." The man called him back. "They're cutting down some trees on the Lewes Road where Colonel Crampthorne's friend is building his new house. If you took a sack with you I daresay the foreman would let you have a bit of brushwood and some sizeable logs as well. He'll be glad to get it cleared away, and the gentleman it belongs to won't miss it. They say he has a lot of money."

"Yes, I've heard about him." The Colonel's friend was an architect and only rich men took up architecture as a profession. "Thank you very much. I'm much obliged to you."

152

The following Saturday he begged the loan of a potato sack from Mr. Twiddle and took it with him to the woods on the Lewes Road and filled it for nothing, and when Christmas came he and Kitty sat by a roaring fire for a night or two, and life took on a more cheerful aspect again.

For Kitty those few days were gilded by an unexpected present that arrived on Christmas Eve. It was a small, square packet, post-marked London and addressed to her in a firm hand-writing that sent the blood to her thin cheeks. Even if Meg had forgotten her, Bob had remembered.

She opened the parcel with tears misting her eyes, and inside she found a shagreen box and a letter.

"*My dear little Kitty,*" Bob wrote. "*Do you remember one wet Sunday afternoon when we were all discussing our favourite nursery rhymes, and you said yours was 'The Little Nut Tree'?* I saw this in a jeweller's window yesterday and thought of you, and in case it is still your favourite rhyme it comes to you with my warmest wishes for a very happy Christmas.

Your affectionate friend, Bob."

Inside the shagreen box, on a white velvet lining, there reposed a tiny jade tree, exquisitely carved, with delicate branches on which were a silver nutmeg and a little gold pear. It was so beautiful that she could have cried with sheer delight. She read the letter again and found a postscript saying that he might be seeing her before long as the parents and Meg were to go to Washington in the New Year and he would be in London on his own. "*So I shall relieve my lonely boredom by visiting Grandmamma.*"

Kitty put the pretty, expensive toy on her dressing-table and every morning when she woke and saw it there she felt comforted, and could forget for a few minutes the worries that pressed upon her.

The sale of the piano saw them well into the New Year, and Kitty had a scrappy letter from Sidney in which he told her that he had passed his finals and could now be addressed as Dr. Burke. He also said that he had been seeing quite a lot of her friend Daisy Drayton, who had developed into a most charming little creature.

Kitty read his letter a little sadly and then wrote to wish him every success, and sent her love to Daisy. The problem of her own employment was becoming more urgent with every day that passed, and she wondered if she could find work serving in a Brighton shop. This suggestion Clara received with the scorn it deserved.

"Don't talk to me about shops!" she sniffed. "You'd be expected to live in, and you'd be 'erded into a room along of a dozen more, and you'd 'ave stale crusts to eat and bad meat. I 'ad a younger sister what died through working in a shop, dear."

"Any anyway there's Johnnie," added Kitty with a sigh. He had settled down happily with Mr. Webber, and he had to have a home and good meal to come back to every night.

"That there Dr. Burke was a bright young spark," Clara said. "Why don't you write to him, dearie, and tell 'im 'ow things are? He might think of something to 'elp you."

But Kitty remembered Daisy and put up her chin. "I'll manage without begging from my friends, thank you, Clara," she said. "Something will turn up."

Clara however had other ideas. The house was getting sadly depleted of its furniture, and now that Effie's little writing-desk had gone the writing materials were kept in a drawer in the kitchen dresser, along with the tradesmen's books, and one day while looking for a bill Clara came across an old address book, in which was the Burkes' address in the Vale of Health.

She pondered over this for some little while, and then after the young people were in bed she began to write a letter to Sidney. It took over a week, because she had not had much schooling, and the result, though it pleased her, caused a little misgiving too in case she had not made the situation clear.

"*miss kitty wont lik me ritin to you mr sidne but i must becorse i shal av to lev ere sun as they wil an eving nose wot they wil do not avin nower to go bar the Workis an ther ma run off to mericky an not writ a word nor sent 1d sinse plese mr sidne cum an elp yrs truly Clara Bucklethorn.*"

But as the days went by and this appeal went unanswered it seemed to Clara that young Dr. Burke had no more interest in his old friends.

January was bitterly cold, with deep snow and a biting wind, and Johnnie took a toboggan up to the woods on a Saturday afternoon to fetch the firewood, but this meant that he came home with scarlet cheeks and an appetite that demanded two eggs for his tea. And then one morning, when a winter's sun was unable to temper a north-east wind, old Lady Winter went to visit an old servant who had been ill, taking her an egg custard and some new-laid eggs and a jug of beef-tea in the shallow basket reserved for such offerings to the sick.

As she was leaving the cottage the woman's husband came in, and the dowager paused to have a word with him.

"Martha seems better today, Ned," she said. "I told her that she is to take every drop of that beef-tea, so mind you see that she does. She needs feeding up."

"Yes, m'lady, thank you. It's very good of you, I'm sure." He hesitated and then went on awkwardly, "I'm glad you came this morning though, m'lady, because there's been something on my conscience like for some time. I hope I did right when I told the lad your ladyship had the wreckage rights along the shore and he'd best get his firewood from the woods, but I've been wondering if he could get up there lately, with the snow being so thick everywhere."

"What lad are you talking about?" Her ladyship paused to draw her sables more closely about her.

"Why, the Ralston lad, m'lady," said Johnnie's friend. "He was collecting driftwood from the shore before Christmas, and when I asked him what he wanted
155

it for he said 'twas for firewood, as they had no coal to spare for their fire."

"What!" Lady Winter stared incredulously. "Young Ralston collecting firewood?"

"Yes, m'lady."

"I never heard of such a thing!" She frowned at the grey sea out in the bay and then with a brief word of thanks and promise that she would look into it, she got into her carriage and was driven away.

Over lunch she asked Miss Booth if she had heard any gossip in the town about the young Ralstons, and learned from her that Mrs. Ralston had run off to America as far back as last July and that the young people had been left with very little money. Mr. Webber had taken the boy into his office, and she had heard that they had been selling furniture to pay their bills.

"But this is disgraceful!" Lady Winter was scandalised and upset. "Why wasn't I told before?" Instead of indulging in her afternoon nap she set off again immediately after lunch for Flint House, where Clara was alone, peeling potatoes for Johnnie's dinner. Kitty was out teaching Mr. Fry's daughters to play the piano, and although she earned a few shillings at it she did not enjoy it very much, because the smell of the rich food in Mr. Fry's ornate house in Prince Albert Road turned her sick and faint.

Clara came up from the basement to answer the groom's knock, wiping her hands on her apron. "Yes?" she said shortly, and then as she recognised the carriage in the road. "Oh, I beg pardon. I didn't see it was 'er ladyship."

"Naturally you won't see who it is unless you open the front door properly," said Lady Winter, marching up the steps and into the hall. Clara shut the door quickly in the face of the groom, while her ladyship stared aghast at the patches on the walls where pictures had been, at the staircase bereft of carpet, the hallway bare of rugs. "Are the bailiffs in?" she demanded.

"No, m'lady." Clara added with more boldness, "Miss Kitty and me is doing our best to keep 'em out."

Her ladyship sniffed. "Well, now I'm here you'd better take me to a room where there is a fire. This hall is icy."

"There's a fire in the kitchen, m'lady."

"Then the kitchen will have to do." The old lady followed her downstairs, and finding that her questions only brought forth reluctant answers, Clara resenting anything akin to what she called "nosey-parkering," she told her to go on peeling the potatoes at the scullery sink. Her ladyship then looked into the stew on the stove and said that it smelt good but needed much more meat in it, and told her how to thicken the gravy with flour, much to her indignation, glanced at some socks that Kitty had been mending and said the darns were better than the socks, and seeing Clara about to wash some greens told her to be sure to see that the water was boiling before she put them into the saucepan, as otherwise they would be uneatable. And as Clara gradually rose to boiling point herself there was a ring at the door bell and she said that would be Miss Kitty.

"Does she usually ring the bell when she comes in?" asked the dowager in surprise.

"No then, she don't," snapped Clara, and as she hurried away her visitor seized the opportunity to glance into the larder and observe its bareness for herself. In the meantime Clara found Dr. Bates on the doorstep.

"I've called to see Miss Kitty," he said brusquely. "I told her to come to my surgery today but she did not come."

"Come to your surgery?" Clara was astonished. "But Miss Kitty is quite well, Doctor."

"I never said she wasn't," said the doctor sharply. "But as she fainted in the grocer's shop yesterday and they sent for me I'd like to be sure that she took my advice before going out today."

"What is this? Kitty fainting!" The dowager suddenly appeared at the top of the basement stairs. "Dr. Bates, did I hear you correctly?"

"You did, Lady Winter." He glanced at her irascibly. "You need not worry about it though. None of Miss Ralston's friends need worry. She is not seriously ill. It is a simple case of malnutrition—or in plain language, starvation. That is all."

"Starvation?" The word was jerked shockingly into the empty hall and the patches on the walls and the bare floor suddenly made sense. Old Lady Winter turned to Clara. "Light a fire somewhere, my good woman, so that the doctor and I can talk."

"I don't light the fire in the morning-room till after tea," said Clara grudgingly. "And then only if Master Johnnie has fetched in some firewood."

"But you can light it now," said her ladyship. "I'll send in some coals tonight."

Clara put a match to the fire and the old lady and the doctor sat by its sulky smoke and talked.

"I'd heard that Mrs. Ralston had gone some time ago," he said. "But it did not occur to me that she would have left the children with nothing. What sort of woman is she?"

"I don't know her," said her ladyship crisply. "And I have never wanted to know her. She is common and—if what one hears about her is true—fast. But talking about her will not help the children. Johnnie, I believe, is working as an office boy with Webber?"

"So I have been told."

"And Kitty has been selling the furniture to buy food."

"If she had, she has not eaten the food herself. She was always a slender little creature, but now she is so thin that you could pass her through a wedding-ring, like one of the best Panama hats!" The doctor exploded wrathfully. "Good God, where were our eyes? We saw her sitting there in church every Sunday, and yet we never saw what was happening under our very noses!"

"I haven't spoken to Kitty in months," said Lady Winter, as distressed as he was. "I was offended because she seemed to avoid me. I blame myself most bitterly for not keeping an eye on her. I could have asked her in to tea, poor child!"

Here Clara came in to say that her ladyship's coachman wanted to know if he was to meet Mr. Bob or let him take a cab from the station.

"Heavens!" Lady Winter looked at the jewelled watch pinned to her coat under the furs. "My grandson is coming to stay for a few days and I had forgotten all about it." She turned to Clara. "Tell them to go and fetch Mr. Bob here if you please, as soon as he arrives." As she went off with the message she told the doctor in a relieved voice, "Bob is a most sensible fellow. I'm glad he is coming. He will tell us what to do. Because we have got to do something...that is very plain!"

The fierceness left the doctor's eyes. Yes, he thought, Bob was a clear-headed young man, and between him and his grandmother the young Ralstons would be in good hands. And he went away to his dog-cart a great deal relieved.

The London train was on time and very soon after it got in Bob ran up the steps of Flint House and into the hall with scarcely a glance for its bareness. He might have been accustomed to his friends' furniture being swept away overnight.

"Grandmamma!" he exclaimed as he was shown into the morning-room where Johnnie's firewood was now blazing away cheerfully. "What on earth are you doing here? And where are Mrs. Ralston and Kitty?"

She told him what she knew. "I'm waiting for Kitty to come in," she finished. "I've just had Dr. Bates here in a rage because the child fainted in the town yesterday through lack of food."

"Lack of *food?*" That any of their friends, and especially Kitty, should be in want of such a commonplace commodity struck Bob as fantastic. "I can't believe it!" He walked to the window and stared down at the wintry garden with its high flint walls. "I did not like Mrs. Ralston, from the little I saw of her while we were here, but I did not think she would desert them, too!"

"What do you mean by that?" His grandmother took

159

him up quickly. "Did the father desert them? Bob, do you know who he is? You needn't keep any secrets from me, my dear. I never did believe in those widow's weeds!"

Bob said slowly: "It was something Richard let out before he left for India...something connected with his brother-in-law."

"With Stephen Ralston Brett?" The old lady's eyes were suddenly bright as bits of gossip came back to her. "Of course! That actress in St. John's Wood...Is he the father, Bob?"

"He may be. I know nothing for certain." He came back to the fire impatiently. "Never mind that now. We have got to plan a campaign to help them before Kitty comes in. Is there any food in the house?"

"Very little. And no coal."

"I'll send some in. I know where the coal merchant is." He was glad to be able to do something to help. "And I'll call at Fry's shop on the way."

"If you please, dear Bob. Order a leg of mutton to be sent here at once, and then go to the grocer's and order cheese and bacon and anything and everything you think they will need. And have it all put down to my account."

"I'll go at once." He shrugged himself into the coat he had just taken off. "But don't you think we ought to take Kitty back to The Gables to be nursed up for a while?"

"The thought had crossed my mind." His grandmother smiled at him affectionately. "The old woman here will look after Johnnie for a few days, I daresay, and he can lunch with us on Sunday. I'll leave a note for him to say what we have done."

As Bob came into the hall the front door opened and Kitty came in and stopped abruptly at seeing him there and caught her breath. And as he saw the sharpened lines of her face and the shadows under her eyes his heart accused him painfully of neglect, and he did not wonder at Dr. Bates's anger.

"Kitty!" he said with gentle reproach, taking her

160

hands in his. "Why didn't you tell me? Why didn't you say in your letter what had happened, so that I could help you?"

"Oh, Bob!" She could not say any more because her throat felt tight and restricted, and he put his arm round her and led her to the morning-room, where the dowager took over the situation from her seat by the fire.

"My dear," she said, "I'm afraid this old house has been showing a very flinty side to you lately, and I want Johnnie to spare you to me for a few days while we decide what is best for you both." And then as Kitty stood in the doorway, struggling with her tears, she added: "You used to play cribbage with me when you came to my house in the old days. Won't you come now, Kitty my love, and play cribbage with me again?"

And as the girl saw the compassion in the kind old face and the tenderness in the understanding eyes, the ice that had bound her heart for months gave way, and she ran to Bob's grandmother and fell on her knees beside her, and as her arms went round her she knew more comfort and security than she had experienced in the whole of her short life.

And Bob, seeing that it was a purely feminine occasion, went out to give his orders in the town. But he did not put anything down to his grandmother's accounts: he paid for it all himself.

As it happened Johnnie was not to spend that night alone with old Clara at Flint House. Just before he got home from the office the front door bell rang once more and Clara found such a smart young man on the doorstep that for a moment she did not recognise him. Then as the light from the hall lamp fell across his smiling face her own cleared.

"Dr. Burke!" she said.

"Well, Clara, so you are still here!" Sidney stepped inside briskly, as one assured of his welcome.

"No thanks to you then!" Clara said indignantly. "I writ that letter to you weeks ago."

"I know, and I would have come sooner, but my father died suddenly in the New Year, and I had to be with my mother for a time." He glanced round at the depleted hall and the jauntiness left him and his blue eyes became troubled. "I can't think why Kitty didn't write and tell me about it herself."

"She was too proud, that was why," Clara said. She led the way to the little morning-room. "Master Johnnie will be in directly, and he's got a good dinner for once. You'd better stay and share it with him."

"But..." Sidney stopped in the act of removing his coat and put his bag down on the floor. "Where is Kitty then?"

"Lady Winter took her off to The Gables just before you came." Clara glanced at him sourly. "Seems she's been fainting in the town through starvation, the doctor says. Well, you can't make a body eat if they won't, can you?"

He asked more humbly if there was a room in the house where he could sleep that night.

"If Miss Kitty were here I wouldn't let you stop," said Clara. "Even if we had a hundred bedrooms, which we ain't. It wouldn't be proper, and there's been enough talk about Flint 'Ouse as 'tis. But Miss Kitty's room is empty, so I'll put clean sheets on her bed for you and you can sleep there."

Johnnie came in at that moment to tell Sidney the latest news of Kitty.

"Bob Winter dropped into the office to tell me where she had gone," he said. "I thought it was jolly decent of him. I'm glad she has gone to The Gables for a bit. You see there's only been my money coming in every week, and seven shillings and sixpence doesn't go very far when there are three people to feed."

Sidney thought it was easy to see why one of the three had refrained from eating and as he sat over dinner with Johnnie and heard more about their struggles since Effie's departure his appetite left him.

When he went up to bed that night in the little room that had been Kitty's he sat for a long time on her narrow bed looking about at the room that was so essentially hers, and in the light of the candles on the dressing-table his dislike of Bob Winter revived. It was like Bob to come and whisk her away like that in the nick of time, just before his own arrival, when he had come especially from London to help her. But he'd been her friend long before the Winters took her up, and in the morning he'd go to The Gables and fetch her, and he'd take her back to his mother to look after. She'd feel much more at home there than with the Winters.

One of the drawers in the dressing-table, emptied in a hurry as Kitty had packed, had not shut properly. He tried to close it and found that it had stuck. Idly he pulled it out and at the back of it, preventing it from shutting, he found a small packet, jammed between the drawer and the back of the chest, and wrapped in yellowed tissue paper. As he removed it the paper fell away and something dropped out and lay on the floor at his feet. He picked it up and it lay there in the palm of his hand: a sugar mouse, its chocolate eyes run to smudges, its paper ears flattened, its string tail eaten by moth, and its sugar hardened into rock.

The candles flickered in the draught from the window, but the wind that rattled the panes was blowing again on the headland in an afternoon in May.

"I'll buy you a sugar mouse," he had said, and he had pulled her hair. Little Sugar Mouse, so grateful for his casual interest, his careless help. But that was before the Winters came to White Cliff Bay, and he had not been able to see her because of Meg....

He heard the hours strike on the morning-room clock down stairs, and dawn was breaking in the sky before he went to bed.

16

After Sunday luncheon at The Gables Bob and his grandmother talked things over with the young Ralstons, offering advice on their future. The luncheon had been excellent, Kitty looked a different creature already for her few days there, and brother and sister sat side by side on a settee in Lady Winter's drawing-room, looking very alike in spite of their different colouring, and oddly determined. They were grateful for all that was being done for them, and anxious to fall in with every suggestion: they agreed that Flint House should be given up and the remaining furniture stored, and they even agreed, reluctantly, to part with Clara as a temporary measure, but when it came to applying to Stephen Ralston Brett for financial assistance they looked at each other, smiled, and shook their heads.

"We shall manage very well without him," Kitty said with a serene certainty that made the old lady cross and brought a smile to Bob's face.

"Don't laugh at them, Bob!" his grandmother said wrathfully, and she stared at Johnnie as if he were to blame for his sister's attitude. "I suppose your friend Dr. Burke had better suggestions to put forward? I notice that he didn't come here with them before he went back to London."

Johnnie said that Sidney had only been able to stay one night.

"Dear Sidney!" Kitty spoke with affection. "It was good of him to come all that way."

Lady Winter did not continue the conversation. Knowing nothing about the sleepless night that the sugar mouse had caused him she thought Dr. Burke an unfeeling young man. The following morning was cold but sunny and she told Bob to take Kitty for a walk and talk some sense into her if he could.

He agreed willingly. As she recovered her physical strength he was discovering a new strength of character that had been missing in the docile child of the old days, and he found it queerly attractive.

The snow had gone from the hills, but it still waited in the hollows under the stunted sloe bushes and in the shadows of the gorse, for more to follow.

"I'll show you the warmest place in White Cliff Bay," he said. "I used to bring my books there in the mornings when you and Meg were at The Laurels." He took her down to the chalky shore under the cliffs, and although the wind above it was bitterly cold, here it was almost as warm as spring. "We'll have to watch the tide," he told her. "And we won't sit under any bulge in the cliff face in case the frost has loosened it and it falls on our heads."

Past falls of chalk had left smooth boulders and Kitty perched herself on one while Bob sat down at her side.

"This is lovely," she said. "I must say I did not feel like climbing the headland just yet. The hot-house atmosphere at The Gables has a peculiarly smothering effect on me. All my arguments seem to be muffled in cotton wool."

"I don't think you should be too independent all the same when there is no reason why you should."

"You agree with your grandmother then, that as we

have a wealthy father Johnnie and I should force him to pay?"

"In a way." He met her clear, direct gaze as directly. "You see, you will marry, Kitty, but Johnnie should have his chance in life. He is too clever a lad to waste the next few years running errands for a lawyer in a little seaside town."

But the little world of White Cliff Bay was beginning to smile on the young Ralstons at last, and being forgiving sort of people, they were prepared to smile back. Ever since it had been learned in the town that Kitty Ralston had been taken up by old Lady Winter again, offers of help had fallen upon her like snowflakes. The Judge's daughters needed music lessons, Mrs. Crampthorne wanted her to have French conversation with a niece who was staying with her, and Miss Grant came in person to beg her to come back to her, as one of her superior young ladies had, in the most reprehensible way, got herself engaged to the curate while taking the children to play rounders on the Recreation Ground.

"So you see, Bob," Kitty told him gravely, "Johnnie and I will be able to keep ourselves quite easily now, if we can find a cottage to rent at a shilling or two a week. We won't starve, Bob dear!...Not again."

"You were starving for weeks," he said reproachfully. "And you never let me know. All I sent you at Christmas was a silly useless toy, when you needed a turkey and a crate of champagne. Why didn't you write to me and tell me how things stood?"

"Perhaps," she said gently, "because I wanted to keep my life with you and Meg—that lovely life that was as fragile and beautiful as your little tree—apart from everything connected with Flint House." She hesitated and then went on courageously: "When I first knew about my father...I felt so soiled and shabby that I wanted to hide from my friends. I can see now that I was wrong: it is stupid to run away from things however terrible they may seem to be." Her chin lifted and a light came into her brown eyes. "So I put it all behind me, and I shut the cupboard door...But I shall always love my little tree. It will stand on my dressing-table for the rest of my life, and when I wake in the mornings I shall see it there, a lovely gesture from one of the kindest friends I have ever known."

"Why do you speak as if everything is over?" he asked, grieved. "Are we friends no longer then, you and I?"

"But of course we are." She turned her head away so that he should not see the tears in her eyes. "Bob, don't misunderstand me over this. That lovely little tree is all part of a fairy tale that I will keep in my heart till I die."

He shook her hand in a firm grip. "You won't shut me out though?" he said urgently. "You won't, will you, Kitty?"

She winked back her tears and managed to smile at him. "No," she promised him. "I will never shut you out again."

He drew a deep breath, squeezed the little hand in his, and got to his feet. "The tide is on the turn, and we must go back." He helped her up beside him. "But before we go, may I not see Fanshawe for you when I return to London next week? Just in case Brett has arranged any financial help for you and Johnnie?"

She hesitated and then she shook her head. "I'd rather you didn't," she said.

"Well?" said the dowager when they returned. "Did Bob persuade you to change your mind?"

Kitty went to the old lady and knelt on the hearthrug at her feet, and the fresh smell of the cold sea air came with her. "Dearest Lady Winter, don't be angry with me, but Johnnie and I can live without assistance from Mr. Brett, and we would like to go on doing it, if you please. All we need to find is a small cottage where we can live on our own."

The dowager was offended. "You don't like it here?"

"On the contrary, I like it too much!" Kitty laughed ruefully. "You know how I love being here, as much as I love you. But the fleshpots are not for me and Johnnie.

We will work for our living because we must, not from choice!"

Lady Winter admired the way the girl refused to call Brett her father, while she could not help deploring her sturdy independence. But Kitty had grown up with a vengeance during the past few months, and now that her eyes had been opened they could not be closed again with appeals to sentiment.

"Well," she said, "if that is how you feel there is no more to be said, is there, Bob?"

"Except," he said, "that I should think a cottage of the sort that Kitty is after ought to be easy to find down here in White Cliff Bay." Over the girl's head his eyes met his grandmother's, and a barely perceptible nod passed between them, and a few days after he had gone back to London Lady Winter took Kitty to see a cottage that belonged, so she said, to a friend of hers.

"It is really only a fisherman's hut," she told her. "A poor shabby place. But if you *must* live like work people I daresay the landlord will let it to you for a nominal rent."

When she saw Kitty's delight in the little place, however, she no longer held out against her, and while the days moved happily towards spring for the young Ralstons in White Cliff Bay, in Hampstead Sidney and his mother examined their slender resources and decided that they would have to move from the Vale of Health.

Sidney began searching for an assistant's post to a country doctor for when his hospital appointment came to an end in three months' time.

"I need more experience," he told his mother one evening flicking over the pages of a medical journal. "And I'm tired of London."

"But what about Daisy?" asked Maidie. "Are you going to desert her?"

"Daisy will not know if I'm here or not," he said quickly. "She has scores of admirers."

"The Draytons are very rich," sighed Maidie.

"Horribly rich. When I've seen how the relatives of some of the poorest patients in hospital deny themselves the ordinary necessities of life so that they can bring little luxuries with them on visiting days, and then I've been to dinner with Daisy's parents and had to eat my way solidly through ten courses, starting with quail and ending with hot-house peaches, I feel myself becoming such a Radical that Keir Hardie would not have me for a friend!"

"I hope you weren't put off your dinner, all the same?"

"Hardly. I like my food too much." He grinned sheepishly and threw the journal aside. "I'd hoped I might have heard from Kitty. I've written to her twice since I went down there, but I suppose the Winters have got her in their clutches again and won't let her go. Bob Winter is an expert at thrusting his oar in where it isn't wanted."

"From what you told me it seemed as if somebody's oar was very much needed," said Maidie gently. "I wish we had not left Kitty and Johnnie alone so long, Sid. They must have thought everybody had deserted them after Effie went."

Sidney scowled at the floor. "I could never stand that chap Winter," he said. "I couldn't see what was so marvellous about him from Kitty's point of view."

"I can," said his mother unexpectedly. "He treated her as if she mattered, for one thing. She used to tell me how kind he was in explaining difficulties in her lessons. She said to me once, 'The nicest thing about Bob is that he always has time to talk to you.'"

"Didn't *I* have time to talk to her then?"

"No," said Maidie honestly. "You did not. When did you put yourself out to be here on the days when she came to us from school? You usually had other fish to fry, and she was only a little schoolgirl that you had known most of your life. On the few occasions when you did condescend to appear your conversation centred on Meg, or on your exploits with other students. You were as cocksure of yourself as you are now, and as convinced that your own future should be as absorbing to others as it was to you. You cannot wonder if the
169

hero of her childhood has been superseded by one less egotistical and more charming."

"Also a great deal wealthier," sneered Sidney.

"That too." His mother smiled consolingly at his angry face. "Cheer up, darling! There's always Daisy."

"Damn Daisy!" exploded Sidney and went off for a walk in the moonlight over the Heath.

Down in White Cliff Bay the Ralstons moved into their cottage on the Harbour Road, and for a fortnight afterwards old Lady Winter visited them every day to make sure that they were able to live on what they had, that Clara was managing the stove without smoking them out, and that Kitty was not being worked to death through the well-meant efforts of her friends. And then, having seen for herself that they had enough food in the larder to last for a week, she went up to London and booked rooms for herself and her companion at a select London hotel that could always be depended upon to welcome her.

On the second afternoon of her visit she told Miss Booth to go and have tea with her married sister in Putney, and in her absence she waited in her private sitting-room for a gentleman to call on her.

Mr. Brett came haughtily, not forgetting the old lady's relationship to his wife, and she greeted him as coldly as the March wind outside.

"First of all I must ask after my great-niece," she said. "How is Muriel?"

He said that she had still not recovered from the boy's birth in the previous September, but that she was cheerful and in good spirits.

"I am glad to hear that." Lady Winter looked at him thoughtfully. "You have quite a large family, Mr. Brett."

"Yes, Lady Winter, I have. Four daughters and one son."

"Is that so? I had heard there were more."

"I beg your pardon?" He stared suspiciously.

"I thought you had five daughters and two sons," she said blandly. "But I may have been misinformed."

"I don't understand you," he said stiffly.

"I think you do, Mr. Brett. Your eldest daughter is nineteen years old—she was at school with my granddaughter Meg. Your elder son, Johnnie, who is nearly fifteen, is working as an office boy in a lawyer's office in White Cliff Bay. Their mother left them with twenty pounds when she went off with Calverley Ricketts last July, and she has not sent them another penny since." She paused and then went on: "Fortunately your children have inherited a great deal of independence from somewhere, and they are now living in a workman's cottage on what they can earn between them." Again she paused, and again he did not answer. He stood there scowling at the fire, his elbow resting on the chimney piece, his well-shod foot on the fender, and she continued abruptly:

"Your son is a fine, honest, open-hearted lad, only anxious to be able to make sufficient income to support his sister. He was Captain of the Eleven and of his school last year, but he has never been entered for a public school and no sum of money seems to have been provided for his further education. I would add that neither he nor his sister know that I have asked you to come here today: they would not willingly touch a penny of your money. But if you consent to advance something for Johnnie I could perhaps persuade him to look on it as a loan, to be repaid when he is able to do so."

After she finished he was silent for so long that she began to wonder if he had been listening to a word of what she had been saying, and then he raised his head and said bitterly: "You make your opinion of me very evident, Lady Winter, but as you appear to know so much I am surprised that nobody saw fit to tell you that I settled a thousand a year upon each child and another on their mother, Effie Fotheringay, when she and I separated some years ago."

"Impossible!" The exclamation was jerked out of the dowager and she apologised. "I beg your pardon, Mr. Brett. I don't doubt your word, but why were the children not told about this? And what in Heaven's name did the mother do with the money, because she spent next to nothing in White Cliff Bay!"

He shrugged his shoulders. "I daresay most of the income went to Ricketts then. He made free with my cigars and brandy in the days when she was living under my protection in Willowbrook Road." He gave her a frosty smile. "The children shall have a letter from Fanshawe in the next day or two, explaining where they stand financially, and until they come of age he will pay their quarterly income to them direct. The capital sum will be theirs of course when they are twenty-one."

"In that case I must apologise." Old Lady Winter held out her hand. "I suppose I should have known you better, Mr. Brett. My remaining task is to persuade those two young people to accept the money."

He barely touched her hand with his. "They may do as they like. It will be there for them, as it always was, if their mother could have kept her thieving hands off it." And he took his leave, as cold and arrogant as when he came.

But as he drove off in the large Talbot behind his chauffeur to see the lawyer, the old lady's picture of Johnnie kept getting between him and the traffic in the streets. That was the kind of son he had dreamed would inherit Cranston, a lad whose school days would have been a source of pride, whose prowess at games would have been something to boast about to friends and acquaintances. Whereas the heir to Cranston had been born with a twisted foot that would never be straight as long as he lived. Delicate and far too uncomplaining for a healthy baby boy, he lay there playing listlessly with his fingers, and only smiling when his four adoring sisters bent over his cot, dangling their long curls for him to catch hold of, and laughing to make him laugh.

As for Muriel she saw no blemish in him. She was sorry about the foot but said lightly that it might have been worse, and was quite content that she had at last done her duty and given her husband a son. Because for Muriel now there could be no more children. Her family and Stephen Brett's was complete, and the irony of it bit into his soul as keenly as the March wind, blowing through his windowless motor car, bit into his proud face.

"I'm sorry for him, but he's a heartless creature all the same," thought the dowager, waiting for her tea to be brought to her in the hotel room. "He cares for nobody but himself—you can see that in his face."

But in this she was wrong. The weak hands of the baby at Cranston had seized hold on Stephen Brett's selfish heart and he could not prise them from it. Every breath he drew, every thought he had, every ounce of love he had ever known, were squandered on the occupant of the cot at The Place. He was never happier than when he had the child in his arms, carrying him on the terrace, or sitting in the library with him on his knee, under Sargent's portrait of the beautiful woman who had given him to him. Nobody else existed in those moments, and even The Place no longer mattered except as an inheritance for his son.

17

It was not easy to convince the young Ralstons that they had the right to the money that their father had settled upon them, and Kitty refused to touch a penny of her portion except as a means for settling her mother's debts. Johnnie, however, presented a more difficult problem, and she found it hard at first to think what she could do for him. He was too old for a public school and too young for a university, but at last Mr. Grant made a suggestion that they thought could be a solution.

There was a parson near Lewes who was a competent coach and took in pupils, his wife looking after the boys like a mother. He had about a dozen pupils in the large Rectory that resembled a Manor House, and Mr. Grant thought he might be persuaded to take Johnnie in the autumn, though he was younger than most of the young men there. The fees were high but he would have the benefit of the big country house and country pursuits. He would be taught to ride and to shoot, and the Reverend Stenhouse belonged to the local hunt. Johnnie, in short, would have a grand time.

When Kitty talked it out with her brother he was willing to fall in with anything that would help his sister and hasten the day when he would be able to support her properly, although he was unwilling to leave her alone at the cottage. But as the weeks went by and summer came they could no longer complain of being friendless, because the residents of White Cliff Bay now vied with each other to show them hospitality, and every week Lady Winter's carriage would visit the cottage with the shallow basket, bringing the first asparagus, or a score of eggs, or a plump chicken for the larder. And as often as Sir Algernon could spare him Bob would visit his grandmother and accompanied the shallow basket if there was a chance of finding Kitty at home.

And then one day when she came in she found Sidney waiting for her.

"Kitty!" he cried. "Sugar Mouse, I've got the most wonderful news!" Still cocksure enough to think that his affairs must be of first consequence to her, in spite of his mother's warning.

She waited smiling, delighted to see him, and ready to rejoice with whatever his news might be.

"Mother and I are coming to live here," he said. "Dr. Bates advertised for an assistant and I saw his advertisement and answered it, and saw him by appointment this morning. I didn't say anything to you in case the post was already filled—didn't want to disappoint you, and Dr. Bates said in his letter that he had several people to see. But he seemed to like me on sight, and I am to start next month when my hospital appointment ends. Mother will come on ahead directly we have found some rooms for her to go to—perhaps in Balmoral House. I see they let furnished lodgings there now."

"And I believe they are very comfortable, too." Kitty took off her hat, tossed it down on the window seat, and made him sit opposite her by the hearth that she had

175

filled with last year's fir cones. "I'm so glad, Sidney dear. It will be very nice to have you and Aunt Maidie here. But what does Daisy have to say to it?"

He frowned, somewhat dashed by her cool kindness. "I don't see what Daisy has to do with it," he said.

She laughed, her brown eyes sparkling with mischief. "I thought your wonderful piece of news was that you were engaged to her!" she said, and he was annoyed that she could treat the prospect so lightly.

"Daisy was almost engaged to a baronet a few weeks ago," he said coldly. "And before that she was trying to make up her mind about a young surgeon with his way to make in the world. She will only get married if she meets a man sufficiently in love with her to make it up for her, and then he'll have to be quick about it or she will change it again before she gets to the altar!"

Kitty laughed again, as happily as before. "It may be your fault that she is so undecided about her admirers," she accused him. "I always thought she fell in love with you when you rescued her that day in London, and she has not fallen out of it since."

He flushed resentfully. "You are quite wrong. Daisy was ready to fall in love with anybody that day—even a policeman."

"Policemen are very nice people," Kitty said. "I've quite an affection for them myself. And Daisy's father is able to put a son-in-law very much on his feet, Sid. You might be able to specialise instead of being an assistant to a country doctor."

"Thank you, but I'd rather start in a country practice and have no father-in-law at all." And Sidney went back to London in a huff.

In July Maidie moved down to Balmoral with her son, and during the next few weeks all the girls in White Cliff Bay developed sore throats and migraine and tennis elbows, so that Dr. Burke had to prescribe for them, until in August the Volunteers pitched their tents in even white lines on the downs behind the town. The Officers' Mess was then inundated with invitations to tennis, croquet and dinner parties, while small informal dances were given in the drawing-rooms there, and the fascination of Dr. Burke's blue eyes was as nothing to the magic cast by the plainest young man in a uniform.

In the last week in August Lady Winter decided to give a ball to the officers of the regiments encamped round about before they left the town. "As Meg is in Washington still," she told Kitty, "it shall be your ball this time, my dear, and yours alone."

Naturally Bob came down from London for it, amused at being eclipsed by the young officers in the Volunteers.

"If there are any Scotsmen among them," he said, "I shall go to bed. There is something about a kilt that is irresistible to the female mind. If my legs weren't so skinny I'd borrow one for the evening."

"You are thinner than you were," said his grandmother with a touch of anxiety. "Is Liz looking after you properly, Bob?"

"She spends her time pressing food on me," he said laughing. "I'm as fit as a fiddle."

"H'm...and how is Sir Algy?"

"Oh, very triumphant because the Government has finally despatched the Channel Tunnel, and now he is even more excited about the Hague Conference banning the dropping of bombs from airships. He doesn't see why the dropping of bombs from flying machines shouldn't come under the ban as well. But that's Sir Algy all over—for ever tilting at windmills." And he went off to superintend the gardeners who were hanging Chinese lanterns and coloured fairy lights in the trees surrounding the lawn.

The drawing-room, converted into a ballroom for the evening, had its long windows thrown open on to the lighted lawn, and when the officers of the various regiments arrived their number far exceeded that of the girls, although they had been invited from miles around, and every young matron in the district had all her unmarried sisters, plain or pretty, to stay the night.

It was the maddest, most glorious night in Kitty's

life, one that she was to look back on with the sure knowledge that such happiness could only come once in a lifetime. She wore the dress she had worn at Meg's ball, and on her shoulder she pinned a spray of the shell-pink roses that Bob brought her when he came to fetch her in his motor car.

"Don't thank me for them," he said. "They come from The Gables hot-houses. And I had a motive for bringing them, because I've got your programme with me, and I've secured six dances. I don't trust these amateur soldiers when they get near a pretty girl."

Feeling slightly breathless Kitty laughed and wondered what old Lady Winter would say, but as it happened the dowager did not even notice that her grandson was dancing rather often with Miss Ralston, because half-way through the evening the officers from the Scots regiments arrived and the girls threw over their partners and danced with them on the lawn, while the pipers took over from the hired orchestra, and Bob sent the waiters flying for more champagne.

As Kitty danced those dances with Bob she was only conscious of his nearness, of the look on his eyes and the warm intimacy of his voice, while he only knew that her dark hair was brushing his cheek, that her feet were light as feathers, and that he did not want to fight any more against falling in love.

Sidney had planned to arrive early that evening, but as luck would have it Dr. Bates was out on a case when an urgent call came into the surgery. By the time he had got back and changed half the night was gone, and he could not see Kitty at The Gables for the crowd in the house and on the lawn. Johnnie, who was happily listening to a group of young men who could not find partners discussing the manoeuvers they had been on the week before, welcomed Sidney absently and told him that Kitty was "somewhere in the garden with Bob, he thought."

Infuriated with the patient who had dragged him off on a case of stomach ache caused by eating too many plums, and further enraged with Bob for having monopolised Kitty now that he was there, and angry with Kitty for not waiting and watching for him, but dancing off with Bob instead, he stalked off in search of them, and came upon them on a rustic seat at the end of the rose-walk.

Bob's arm was round Kitty's waist and he did not remove it as Sidney approached but looked up lazily with a grin of welcome, while Kitty herself scarcely seemed to see him for a moment. Then she glanced shyly at Bob, her lips framing a question, and as he nodded, she held out her hand and cried softly: "Sid, my dear, you shall be the first to know! Oh Sidney, Bob and I are engaged to be married... and I'm the happiest girl in the world!"

The engagement was a nine days' wonder in the town, but congratulations poured in from all sides, while from Washington came a cable of delighted welcome, followed by letters from Meg and her parents, saying that as Kitty was almost one of the family already it was only natural for Bob to have chosen her. Sidney remarked sourly to his mother:

"Funny thing, I'd have thought the great Winters would have objected to having Kitty as a daughter-in-law."

Maidie regarded her son thoughtfully. "Now why should you think that?" she asked.

"Well..." He flushed darkly, remembering Richard's remarks about Effie. "I suppose some people might consider her to be a nobody."

"They might," agreed Maidie. "But we wouldn't, would we?"

Sidney said he had a patient to see. "I shall be glad when the plum season is finished," he grumbled. "Half the kids in the town have stomach ache from gorging themselves on plums and green apples."

"Dr. Bates says you can never keep boys away from orchards," said Maidie. "As long as there are plums and green apples he reckons they will steal them and suffer for it."

Sidney carried his resentment about Kitty's engagement back with him to the surgery, where Dr. Bates was mixing a cough mixture for a chronically bronchial patient.

"H'm." The doctor held up the medicine bottle to the light from the window, shook it and filled it with water from the dispensary tap. "It surprises you, does it, that Sir Arthur has welcomed Kitty as a bride for his only son?"

"Yes," said Sidney unhappily. "It does."

"It shouldn't," said Dr. Bates with his usual brevity. "If you use your eyes." And with this cryptic remark he corked the bottle, clapped a label on it, wrapped it in white paper and sealed the ends with speed born of practice, and went out to give it to the old gentleman in his waiting room.

Dr. Burke had no idea what he meant and he did not much care. He felt sore and angry, and having a few hours off that afternoon, he struck up the headland for a walk and came to the spot at the top where he had sat with Kitty on that far off afternoon in May, and looked down on the town.

So cocksure he had been in those days, with a conceit that was only now beginning to sicken and die. When Kitty had tried to explain what the isolation of the headland meant to her he had asked carelessly if it made her feel like God, and she had replied no...like Gulliver. He saw those two attitudes of mind now clearly for the first time: his own arrogance and her humility. Even then he was a god, astride his world, while she was Gulliver, imprisoned and surrounded by little, puzzling people.

He had called her a sugar mouse, seeing in her a nice child, mouse-like and inoffensive, and when he met the Winters he had deserted her for Meg. He thought with shame of the dance at the school, to which he had been invited as Kitty's guest, and which he had passed almost entirely in Meg's company, and he remembered later occasions when Meg had used him for her own amusement, while all the time Kitty was there, growing up, her clear brown eyes comparing him with Bob from under her cloud of dark hair.

In the toy station far below a clock-work train was getting up steam: he could see its tiny puff of smoke and the arm of the signal at the end of the platform, while out on the Harbour Road a toy motor-car was making its way towards a fisherman's cottage. The white tents had gone from the hills behind the town, and the girls of White Cliff Bay were down there somewhere, playing disconsolately on tennis courts depleted of bronzed young men, and wondering what had become of Dr. Burke.

"Oh, Sugar Mouse!" groaned Sidney from the imprisoning wind up on the headland. "What a stupid, blind, *bloody* fool I've been!"

Kitty insisted on continuing her work for Miss Grant, in spite of the diamond hoop on her finger, and that September Johnnie joined Mr. Stenhouse's establishment. He had rather lost his enthusiasm for the Volunteers on learning that Mr. Haldane was thinking of re-naming them the Territorial Army, to be used only for home defence in time of war.

Bob had returned to London, but seized every excuse to visit The Gables as November approached and the mists of autumn turned the smoke of London to choking, yellow fog. It was on one of these visits towards the end of November that Dr. Bates was called in a hurry to The Gables. Surgery hour was nearly over when he returned, and Sidney was surprised that he should have been so long.

"Did the old lady have a heart attack?" he asked.

The doctor looked at him as if he did not hear what he said and Sidney repeated his question.

"No," said the old man then. "It was nothing to do with Lady Winter. It was her grandson...young Bob." He put down his bag rather wearily as if it held a heavy weight. "The poor chap's had another hemorrhage."

"A hemorrhage?" Sidney's heart missed a beat. "What do you mean, sir?"

181

"What I say." The doctor lowered himself into his worn arm-chair and began to unlace his boots. "He had one some years ago when he was a lad at school. He was sent down here then for fresh air, good country food, no exertion—you know the treatment—and seemed better for it, and it was thought that the damage was healed. But there is no real cure for the damned thing, whatever these specialists say. You could tell that by looking at the boy."

Sidney remembered the old doctor's advice to him to use his eyes, and suddenly he recollected certain damning things that he had paid little attention to at the time because his jealousy for Bob had blinded him. The grip of his hand, hot and dry, the little cough, the high colour on his cheek-bones...

"Phthisis," he muttered, his thoughts with Kitty. "It can't be..."

"Phthisis it is," said Dr. Bates grimly.

"But...he can't marry!" Sidney flushed under the keen eyes of his employer. "It isn't fair on Kitty!"

"Who are we to say what is fair on Kitty?" demanded Dr. Bates. "If she wants to marry him and he can be persuaded to let her, then don't let us deny them a fleeting happiness." He got up from the leather chair, and as he passed his young assistant on his way to his consulting room he said in a voice almost too low for him to hear, "I give them two years..."

Paris was now out of the question for Bob: the doctors suggested Davos or South Africa, and Kitty did not care which it was to be, as long as she could be with them. It never occurred to her that she should not marry him, and when he suggested they should wait a time she had laughed and told him not to be silly.

"You got better six years ago," she told him gaily. "You'll get better now. So we'll say no more about *that!*"

And so, directly he was strong enough, they were married quietly in White Cliff Bay, with Johnnie to give his sister away, and only a handful of friends at The Gables afterwards to wish them luck before they left for Switzerland. Bob's parents and Meg had not

been able to leave Washington in time for the cere-
mony.

As Sidney said goodbye he told the radiant little
bride, "If there is anything I can do, Kit, at any time,
you have only to send for me and I'll come."

"Dear Sid!" She put her hand in his in the old affectionate way and just for a moment a shadow touched
the happiness in her eyes. "Look after Johnnie for me,
Sid...only look after Johnnie!"

And then she was gone.

18

White Cliff Bay did not change much in the next five years. In the April of 1912 it was a bleak and ugly as ever, residents as few, the summer visitors as constant in their stay in the little town.

In the summer of 1910, just after King Edward died, Dr. Bates took young Dr. Burke into partnership, the death of the monarch reminding him that he was not getting any younger.

"I've nobody to leave my money to," he explained when Sidney protested that he had nothing to put down for his share of the practice. "A childless old widower like me doesn't need more than he has already. I have my house and garden, and the garden is my delight. The more work I can persuade you to take off my shoulders, the more time I shall have to spare for my plants and my greenhouse. You have almost doubled the practice since you have been here, too, so that I think we can call it quits."

Maidie was delighted when he accepted the offer. "It may be only a country practice," she said, "but it is a good one, Sid. And it's all you need... except a wife. You'll be able to marry now, my love."

"But haven't I got a mother to look after me?" he demanded. "What do I want with a wife?"

"It's not the same thing at all," Maidie said severely. "And out of pity to the young women of White Cliff Bay I think you should put them out of their misery, now that the only curate is married. Once the news of this partnership leaks out they won't leave you alone." She paused. "Mind you, some girls do need a little encouragement. You haven't had any letters from Daisy lately, I've noticed."

"As I haven't written to her, that is scarcely surprising. And I cannot see what Daisy has to do with what we were discussing. I think I shall buy a motor car."

And buy one he did, and for a time the town suffered from a spate of drunken lamp-posts, leaning this way and that, but the older inhabitants, most of whom were Dr. Bates's patients, merely shrugged their shoulders and remarked that "they reckoned young Dr. Burke had been taking his moty-car out again."

Whether he found the motor-car a good substitute for a wife his mother never knew, but it is certain that he cherished it almost as tenderly, and that he was still unmarried on that April morning in 1912, when he was up so early that Clara had not even had time to do her daily rubbing up of the brass plate on the railings by the gate.

The house that Sidney had rented for his mother over the past five years was small but compact, and cottage in appearance, and she liked it because it reminded her of the happy days she had spent in the Vale of Health, and as a rule her son enjoyed a fairly leisurely breakfast with her before starting off for the surgery in Broad Street.

But this morning Clara had scarcely set the bacon on the table before the car was out of the garage, and Sidney was making sure that the petrol tank—cunningly hidden under the cushion in the driver's seat—

was filled with petrol, and that there was sufficient water in the radiator.

"What time does the boat get in?" asked Maidie from the open dining-room window, as she watched him peering anxiously into the intestines of the car.

"She should dock at nine, but you know what these Channel steamers are." Sidney wiped his hands on a piece of rag and threw it into the back of the car, along with a wooden box of tools, a couple of spare tyres, and a gallon tin of petrol that had splashed over on to the rubber mat.

"And where," asked Maidie, grimly regarding all this clutter, "is the precious baby and his nannie going to sit?"

Sidney grinned. "Oh, The Gables' carriage is being sent for them. I arranged it with the coachman yesterday. I told him that I would fetch Kitty, and I don't think he liked it."

"I don't suppose he would. After all if she wrote from Switzerland telling him to meet the boat this morning, and the poor man finds that he is only to be allowed to drive the baby and its nannie home for the first time, one cannot blame him for not liking it."

"I've got something to say to Kitty," Sidney said obstinately. "And I've waited five years to say it."

"Dear little Kitty!" Maidie sighed. "I wonder what she feels like, coming back to White Cliff Bay as owner of The Gables? I don't suppose she ever thought old Lady Winter would leave it to her."

"The dowager was a wise old bird," said Sidney. "I got quite attached to her in the end. She told me once that she thought Kitty needed something to protect her from Bob's family: I daresay that was why she left her the place, so that it could act as a buffer between her and her in-laws."

"But it won't keep them out," said Maidie smiling. "Miss Grant told me that Sir Arthur is waiting impatiently to see his grandson and that he and Lady Winter plan to come and stay at The Gables next month." Her son took no notice and she went on after a moment.

186

"Kitty is not like Meg, Sid. She won't forget poor Bob in a hurry, and if I were a young man who thought seriously of putting my fate to the test with her I wouldn't rush my fences."

"Wouldn't you then?" Sidney glanced at his hands and said he had just time to wash before he started. He went up to his room and Maidie followed him.

"I've been wondering," she said, "if Kitty has seen any English newspapers in the last few days?"

"Why should she?" He poured cold water into his basin and began to scrub his hands.

"Well... about the *Titanic*, dear!"

"Oh, that! I should say she had seen it. It was widely reported in the foreign papers." Sidney's voice was careless as he concentrated on getting his hands clean.

"I'm talking about the passenger list, Sid. The Bretts were on that ship."

"The Ralston Bretts, do you mean?" He took his towel and began to dry his hands and arms energetically.

"Yes. Stephen Brett, his wife, and their little son."

"Indeed? Then I hope Kitty won't have seen it." He threw the towel on to the bed, came to his mother and kissed her, and ran downstairs whistling softly, to the motor car. She heard a back-fire or two as he cranked it up and then it went chugging down the road towards the Harbour.

Maidie went back to the little parlour that she had turned into a drawing-room and found yesterday's paper that Clara had tidied away in the bamboo rack. She opened the paper and found the final lists of victims again and the few lines that the Ralston Bretts had been given beneath it. "Among those who perished were Mr. and Mrs. Ralston Brett of Cranston Place in Norfolk and their little son. Mr. Brett's death and that of the little boy means that The Place, which had been in the family for four centuries, will now pass to his cousin, Mr. Lionel Brett, as Mr. Ralston Brett had no other sons. We understand that the child had been deformed from birth, and Mr. Brett was taking him to see

187

an American surgeon who has performed miracles with crooked limbs in children."

No other sons...Maidie's thoughts went to Johnnie, enjoying to the full his first year at Oxford. Had Stephen never given a thought for him when he had arranged that voyage on what was said to be an unsinkable ship, for his little crippled heir?

The Bretts were far from Sidney's mind as he waited for the boat to dock and saw Kitty there, her slight, black-clad figure standing out among the group of first-class passengers at the rails. She saw him and waved, and turned to the child in its nurse's arm beside her and made him wave, too. The little boy did so gravely, his eyes looking about him to discover the person whom his mother was so anxious that he should greet.

"Sidney!" Kitty said in her old glad way as they came from the Customs sheds to where he was waiting for them. "This is a lovely surprise!...and that is the famous motor car we heard so much about! Is it quicker than the carriage?"

"It doesn't often break down." There was a gleam of his old mischief in the blue eyes. "Will you trust yourself to it, Kitty, or do you prefer the carriage?"

She hesitated, unwilling to hurt his feelings, and equally unwilling to hurt the kind old servants in the carriage. "I'll come a little way with you," she said. "We'll wait for the carriage to pick me up before it turns down into the town. I've so much to say to you, but there won't be time to say it all today."

She greeted the coachman and the groom, introduced the little boy to them, and much to their satisfaction said that she would wait for them on the Harbour Road, and then, having seen the child and his nurse safely bestowed, she climbed into the motor car beside Sidney, tied a veil round her hat and accepted Maidie's goggles and the rug that he wrapped round her knees, and they started off.

She asked after his mother as they left the harbour behind and he remembered the *Titanic*. He asked her if she had seen the passenger lists.

"Yes." Her voice was quiet and unemotional. "It's extraordinary that I cannot feel the slightest grief for my father. I have been feeling rather guilty about it."

"You needn't, surely? He didn't treat you very well."

"Even so, one would have thought the ties of blood and affection would still exist somewhere in me. But they don't."

"That is not your fault."

"But he couldn't have inspired love in nobody? There were those little girls...But I daresay their grandmother will have them to live with her at the Dower House. I think they were more often with her than at The Place. And Richard will be glad that Lionel is to be at Cranston now. He always liked him."

They came to the cottage where she had lived with Johnnie and she said she was keeping it for Clara. "For when she gets too old to work for your mother any longer. She will have her ten shillings a week old age pension, you see, and she might let a room in the summer to help out." After a moment she added softly, "I never knew that Bob had bought that cottage for me until he gave me the deeds on our wedding-day!"

They were approaching Flint House and she asked him to slow down and as she read the notice "Apartments to Let" she gave a small grimace.

"So that's what it has come to, poor old Flint House! Let's stop and wait for the carriage here, Sid."

He pulled up just beyond the house and she removed the disfiguring goggles and veil and glanced at him affectionately, and then at the shadows of the clouds that were racing across the white-crested sea.

"My lack of affection for my father is all the more extraordinary to me," she said less tranquilly, "because when Bob died I felt the end of my world had come."

"If it would help to tell me about it," he said. "I'm here, Sugar Mouse."

She smiled at the familiar name. "Dear Sid!" she said. "Always such a friend!" It was not what he wanted to hear but he let it pass, and presently she continued with a grief in her eyes and her voice that was too deep for tears, "We had been in Davos for two years when...my darling seemed to recover. The doctors thought that the scarred lungs had healed, and so we took a villa in Italy and lived there for a wonderfully happy year. Robbie was born, and I cheated myself into believing that the wretched disease could be cured after all. And then, when Robbie was six months old, it started up again, and we returned to Davos, and I was told there was no hope." Her eyes left the sea and went to the white cliffs and the familiar outline of the headland, and the grey Martello Tower at its foot. "Sid, will they ever be able to cure it, do you think?"

"I would say that a cure will be discovered some day," he said. "There was an old boy who used to lecture to us at college and he said that if you could give a chap a year to live you could give him ten, or a lifetime. And new discoveries in medicine are being made every day. If it's any comfort to you, Kitty, my dear, Bates gave Bob two years when you married him...and you had five. Which rather bears out the theory of the old boy in college."

"Five years is so short a time when you love a person as I loved Bob," she said. "So very short...There never was anybody like him, and there never will be again. I can't tell you how brave he was at the last...I shall never forget it or him."

He wanted to say that she was young, and that she would marry again, but the words would not come, and he wondered if his mother had been right when she said that Kitty was not like Meg: once she gave her heart it was for always. The sea was suddenly dark with a cloud that crossed the sun and the April wind was chill.

Far behind them the speck that was the carriage had separated itself from the harbour and the sheds and the funnels of the steamer behind it, and was slowly taking shape on the Harbour Road. If he wanted to say what he had to say then he must be quick, or the moment would be gone. "Don't rush your fences," Maidie had said, and now for the first time, he was inclined to agree with her.

So, wisely he sat silent, and as they waited for the carriage he had the feeling that the old deep companionship of that far-off day on the headland was back with them, and that they understood each other better than they had done in years.

"I'd hoped you would marry Daisy," Kitty said gently. "She is a dear little creature, Sid, and would have made you a splendid wife."

"She is making somebody else a splendid wife," he told her gravely. "And I am very happy for him and for her."

She glanced at him with a hint of perplexity. He had changed a lot since she had been away: there was a new strength of purpose and a steadiness in him that had been lacking before. She put her hand lightly on his arm. "Dear Sid!" she said. "How nice it is to have you with me again!"

He looked at the small gloved hand and wanted to raise it to his lips. He would have liked to make an extravagant gesture but extravagance and gestures were out of place. The inborn dignity that had matured in her would not allow it, and before he could speak she took her hand away.

"Here they are!" she cried smiling. She got out of the motor car and waited for the carriage to draw up beside them, the coachman pulled in the horses, the groom sprang down and opened the door, and helped her to climb up beside the nurse. Sidney saw the child move over at once to his mother's lap, and as Kitty's cheek brushed his head caressingly, Bob's eyes looked out of the little boy's face at him gravely and wonderingly before they drove on.

"Nasty, unreliable contraptions, them moty cars, ma'am," said Nannie severely. "You was wise not to go further in it."

"Yes," said Kitty serenely. "I think I was."

Standing by his despised motor car Dr. Burke watched the carriage until it was out of sight, and then he walked across the road to the beach and went down on the shingle and made his way to a break-water and sat there for a time.

The confiding child that had been Kitty had gone long ago, and the romantic girl with her head in the stars had followed her when Bob died, but the young mistress of The Gables, driving back now to take up the reins where old Lady Winter had let them fall, had a beauty of spirit that was unique: if he could not have her for his wife he would have no other.

He plunged his hand into his pocket and took from it a small parcel that he had intended to show her that day, only somehow he had forgotten it and now it was too late. He held it in his hands and smiled a little wryly, a little sadly, for the sentimentality that had made him keep it. Then he wrapped it tighter in its yellowed tissue paper, and getting to his feet he threw it as far as he could into the sea.

The paper unwound from the sinking weight of sugar and floated for a moment on the surface of the water, and then a wave covered it and it was gone.

Far away on the horizon the sunshine had come back in a band of gold across the shadowed sea, widening as it travelled slowly towards him, and it seemed to him in that moment that the future might be like it, as warm and as golden, if only he had the patience to wait.